STING

JUDE WATSON

STI

NG

It takes a crook to catch a crook

Scholastic Press / New York

All rights reserved. Published by Scholastic Press, an imprint of Scholastic Inc., *Publishers since 1920.* SCHOLASTIC, SCHOLASTIC PRESS, and associated logos are trademarks and/or registered trademarks of Scholastic Inc.

The publisher does not have any control over and does not assume any responsibility for author or third-party websites or their content.

This book is a work of fiction. Names, characters, places, and incidents are either the product of the author's imagination or are used fictitiously, and any resemblance to actual persons, living or dead, business establishments, events, or locales is entirely coincidental.

Library of Congress Cataloging-in-Publication Data available

ISBN 978-0-545-86346-9

10 9 8 7 6 5 4 3 2 1   16 17 18 19 20

Printed in the U.S.A.   23
First edition, September 2016

Book design by Nina Goffi

TO EVERY KID WITH AN OVERACTIVE IMAGINATION

"The place in which I'll fit will not exist until I make it."
— James Baldwin

BEFORE

BLOOD RED STAR

Best place to hide? In plain sight. Every thief knows that.

It was broad daylight, but the thief wore a disguise: a uniform. In a rented estate for billionaires, nobody notices the help.

The grand redbrick mansion was nestled in the rolling green hills of Virginia, where the meadows were sweet, the mists were gentle, and the power brokers of Washington, DC, were only an hour away, waiting to be bribed. Exactly why billionaires all over the world flocked here.

The thick gray carpet reduced footsteps to whispers. The thief moved quickly down the corridors and fit the key into the lock, then pushed open the door to the library.

Sunlight streamed in through double-height windows and cast squares of rich gold on the carpet. Outside, roses tumbled, impossibly lush, their thick heads almost too heavy for their stalks. Even the bees appeared fat and prosperous, lumbering from bloom to bloom and occasionally blundering against the window with a dull thwack.

Safecracking was not at the top of the thief's skill set. But this job was worth the risk. If there were three wheels in the wheel pack, cobalt plates, and relockers, it would take too much time. The thief would have to resort to a drill and a borescope. Doable, but there would be noise.

The safe was behind a painting. Such a cliché. The thief flipped back the heavy, gilded frame.

It was amusing that people thought safes were, well, *safe*, when any safe was vulnerable to the right thief with tools and enough time. When it came to safes, the enemy was not the lock, not the steel, not the combination — only time.

The house staff ran on a strict schedule. The landscape workers would be moving to the flower gardens next. The thief had twelve minutes.

Opening the safe took ten.

A carved box sat alone in the safe. An aroma rose from the wood — something familiar, sweet and spicy, like a Christmas cookie. The thief reached in and opened the box, only to find another. Then another. With mounting exasperation, three more times the thief opened a slightly smaller box, stacking them and pushing them aside until the seventh box remained.

Gloved fingers itching with anticipation, the thief raised the lid.

The thief's breath caught. Three perfect star sapphires of a shade somewhere close to heaven. For a moment, maybe a trick of the light, the crystal star that flashed in the deep blue was bloodred.

The thief scooped them into a palm. Felt their unusual coldness.

Light dimmed as though a transparent veil had dropped between this room and the world. All air and sun sucked out of the space, replaced by an oily darkness. Like a frozen midnight river and no air to breathe . . .

The thief felt something — a shove? — as some . . . *thing* seemed to brush by.

Cold fear paralyzed bone and muscle.

The thief stood, frozen, and saw a sudden steaming at the window, as if someone had breathed against it.

Then an image of two hands appeared against the glass, a spreading imprint of palms and fingers.

As if someone were desperate to get out.

Get out get out get out.

Panic rushed through the thief. The jewels fell onto the carpet, knocking against one another.

And then the handprints faded, light flooded back in, and the thief could breathe again.

Outside? Just sunshine and air and grass and roses.

Heart slamming, the thief pushed away what had just happened, chalked it up to nerves and no breakfast, and fumbled for the stones.

Steady hands now trembled as they stacked the empty boxes inside one another. The safe door closed, the tumblers clicking, locked once again.

Out the door again, closing it quietly. Moving swiftly, reassured by solid wood, plaster walls, an air conditioner's hum. Normal things. Not thinking about the dead weight in a pocket, about the imprint of two palms on foggy glass.

The door. The thief had forgotten to lock the door.

Well. Somebody else's problem.

The thief's partner came down the hallway on schedule.

All okay?

Slight change of plan. You stash the loot.

That's not the plan.

That's why it's called change.

The thief handed over the stones and was gone.

The disappearance of one of the workers would be noted.

Likewise the fact that a locked door was now open. Questions would be asked. But the thief's partner would have to deal. The thief had never felt nerves like this before. Hands that trembled, knees like water, legs that shook.

The thief hurried across the lawn, grateful for sunshine, and feeling that something dark and evil had been left behind.

1

NOW

BACK AGAIN AND
UPSIDE DOWN

Paris, France

March McQuin didn't think he'd ever be in this position
again — upside down and dangling twenty feet over a stone
floor at three o'clock in the morning.

It was awesome.

If only he didn't have an incredible urge to sneeze.

March closed his eyes, pressed his lips together, and
swallowed — his usual remedy against avoiding an explosive
spew of noise, spit, and snot. Dust filled his nose, the kind of
ancient grime that tends to layer on the gutters and skylights
of Parisian rooftops.

Instead of a sneeze, what emerged sounded like an ele-
phant strangling on a trumpet.

The voice came through his earpiece. "What was that?"
their lookout, Darius Fray, asked.

"I sneezed," March whispered.

"Next time do it louder. I don't think they heard you in
London."

"You know, a simple gesundheit would do."

"Yeah, that and some earplugs."

His twin sister, Jules, glanced at him, her wide eyes tele-
graphing a clear message: *Shut up.* Their mark, Yves
Beaumarie, was snoozing away down the hall. Their source
had promised that he took a sleeping pill every night, but
March's father, the world-famous and unfortunately deceased

cat burglar Alfie McQuin, had always said, *Never trust a source 100 percent. Or even ninety. Okay, 75 percent, tops.*

There was no question they were rusty. They hadn't pulled a job in over a year. But this job was supposed to be super easy. *A cakewalk*, Hamish Tarscher had said.

What the heck is a cakewalk?

Focus, March.

Jules swung by her knees, taking photos of the security panel. The house was built in the seventeenth century, but the mark liked contemporary design. He'd gutted the old woodwork and exposed all the piping and ducts. March thought it was hideous, but it gave his twin plenty of options to display her abilities on her aerial silks — flexible fabric upon which she could twirl, fly, and suspend herself by her ankles in midair. March might look like a trussed-up turkey on the silks, but Jules looked like an acrobatic angel.

His twin had studied trapeze and gymnastics, had been a street performer since she was five, back before he knew her. He couldn't say she'd taught him everything she knew, because he didn't know how to twirl by his ankles, and he didn't want to learn. But he knew enough not to fall and wait for Jules to do the hard stuff.

He hung on a pipe and waited. He could hear Izzy Mercado's small, steady voice in his earpiece, rapping out instructions on how to bypass a panel.

Jules dropped down, now hanging by her knees, and keyed in some numbers. She was disabling the thing *upside down.*

It's not like he'd tell her or anything, but his twin was amazing.

March saw the light flash green.

Jules did a double somersault on her way down to the floor. Show-off.

March used the silks to propel him into an awkward half somersault and landed on one foot before crashing to his knees.

Jules rolled her eyes.

"You in, bro?" Darius asked. "I don't hear an alarm, but remember, you busted my eardrum before."

"In," March whispered. "Going silent now."

This was the charged moment he loved. The first release of pressure, when you were in, with the security disabled, and all that was ahead was grabbing the loot and making the getaway. He'd *missed* this.

This moment was when all the planning was worth it. March had gone over the details of this heist until it was in his dreams and included a clown.

Housekeeper away, the mark in a deep sleep, a briefcase full of loose diamonds. *You see me, Pop? That was one perfect entry. If ever there was a sure thing, this is it.*

March often talked to Alfie in his head. The trouble was, his pop talked back.

Haven't I taught you anything? Never trust a sure thing.

2

SOMETHING COLD,
SOMETHING BLUE

March pressed his fingers against his forehead. Telling his dad to shut up was definitely not cool when he was alive. But there was one advantage to his being dead.

Sorry, Pop, you're dead. Shut up already.

Jules nudged him. "Wake up, dream boy," she whispered. "You got me into this. Let's go steal some diamonds."

She pointed to a long, industrial-looking desk against one wall. The briefcase was right where it was supposed to be.

Beaumarie had decided to sell his family jewels. He had a serious gambling habit, and it didn't help that he lived next door to a posh gambling club. He was scheduled to meet a diamond dealer tomorrow at the Bristol, a swanky hotel.

It took March only thirty seconds to pick the lock on the briefcase. It was a standard lock, which meant it was a joke. All it took was a slender shim and the right touch.

He'd been picking locks since age four. When Alfie wanted him to be quiet, he'd dump a bunch of locks on the kitchen table, set a timer, and hand March a shim.

March opened the case, Jules at his shoulder. The briefcase was lined with velvet pouches. He picked up one and shook a stone into his palm.

It felt so cold.

It wasn't a diamond. It was a large sapphire, royal blue, with a star in the center. It mesmerized him for a moment, pulling him into a whirling cosmos of deep blue starlight. Yet at the same time he felt as though a sudden rush of eternity blew through him, an empty black void that moved like an oily, cold river. Sudden panic rippled through him, and he felt his throat close. He had to fight the desire to toss the jewel back into the pouch.

Then he heard the noise. Someone stirring in the bedroom off the hall.

He and Jules froze. He shoved the stone in his pocket while Jules snapped the briefcase closed. March almost moaned as the beautiful pouches full of loot disappeared.

They slid behind the couch. If Yves was coming out for cookies and milk, they were toast and jam.

Jules grabbed his arm as they heard a tapping noise. March grinned. He knew what this was.

Paws on a stone floor. They knew everything about their mark, including how much Monsieur Yves Beaumarie doted on his small, ugly dog.

They stood as the brown dog trotted toward them, ears twitching, stumpy tail wagging. She was small enough to fit in a purse, but squat and pudgy, with a long snout. March bent down, reaching into one pocket for a dog treat. He almost passed out from the dog breath that emanated from the panting animal. He held out the treat, and the dog sniffed it before gobbling it down and immediately sniffing for more.

"Good girl, La Rochelle," March murmured. M. Beaumarie had named the dog after his favorite vacation spot in France. Nosing for more, the dog nipped his finger. "Ow!"

"Shhh," Jules warned. "Something's wrong."

"I know. She really stinks. Ow!" March cried as La Rochelle bit the hand that fed her.

"Not the dog! There's a noise on the roof," Jules whispered.

"Wind."

"There wasn't any wind tonight," Jules said.

From the high window, a beam of light moved over the room. Heart pounding, March hit the floor the same time as Jules. They squirmed away from the light and crawled fast down the hall. La Rochelle thought it was a game and nipped at March's heels. Her stumpy legs revolved, trying to catch up with them. She gave a playful growl.

"Shhhh," March said, digging in his pocket for another treat. He threw it toward the bedroom, and she skittered toward it.

A faint, high noise could be heard. March knew that noise. Someone was slicing through the ornate grillwork.

Someone *else* was breaking into the apartment!

3

DOG BREATH

March's heart leaped and twisted like a fish caught on a line. He shot a panicked look at Jules.

Jules pointed toward the bedroom.

They glided through the doorway, their knees whispering against the hard floor. La Rochelle waddled after them, sniffing at March's pants. The man in the bed sighed and flopped over. He was dressed in silk pajamas and wore a sleep mask. March and Jules rolled under the bed. March banged his head on the wooden frame. His heart sped up to cardiac arrest levels.

Yves Beaumarie smacked his lips. *"Mon chou,"* he murmured in his sleep.

My cabbage? March wondered.

Suddenly a hand flopped down by the floor. "La Rochelle . . ." Beaumarie murmured. *"Mon petit chien . . . où es-tu?"*

The hand groped along the floor. Beaumarie was starting to wake up, concerned about his dog. There was only one thing to do.

March slithered closer. He steeled himself. It was either this or prison.

He leaned over and licked the man's hand.

Jules clutched her throat, pretending to gag.

Beaumarie let out a sigh. *"Ah! Mon ange!"*

He was calling that stinky mutt an angel! Settling back into sleep, Beaumarie flipped over and began to snore.

March blocked out the chain saw as best he could. He could hear the sounds of stealth — the smallest of sounds. Footsteps padding across the floor. A slight rustling. And then the unmistakable snap of a briefcase lock. March gave an anguished look at Jules. Someone was stealing their diamonds!

March put his mouth close to Jules's ear. "At least we're safe," he whispered.

That's when an alarm went off.

4

THE BEST EXIT IS UP

La Rochelle howled. Beaumarie sat up in bed. He fumbled for a light but forgot he was wearing a sleep mask. He bumped his head on the headboard and swore.

No time to think, no time to make a plan. March and Jules scrambled out from under the bed and ran. Whoever had been in the house was gone, the briefcase open and empty, the window still open.

Lights snapped on in the kitchen.

"Monsieur BeauMARIE!" The voice was high and panicked. Rapid French followed, too fast for March to translate. It was the housekeeper, the one who was *supposed* to be on holiday in Brittany, thank you very much, Hamish!

"*La police!*"

That he understood.

Jules was already moving, running and slipping her silks out from her waist pack at the same time. Before March could take another breath she'd swung the silk over the metal duct overhead.

"Move!" she hissed.

March scrambled up the silk. His blood thundered in his ears. He may have missed the excitement of the life of a thief, but he didn't miss the panic. As soon as he'd climbed on top of the duct, Jules climbed up, faster and more agile than he. She rolled up the silk and then tightrope-walked along the ductwork as he crawled behind her. Jules reached the open window and stuck one foot out.

The stout housekeeper galloped into the space below, brandishing a copper tray.

Jules half turned, one leg out the window. "What is she going to do, serve us up with the turnips?" she asked.

Now that they were almost out, March let himself snort a laugh. "We're in France. She'll need some parsley."

The housekeeper let the round tray fly. It spun in an aggressive, perfect arc, straight toward him. He could only stare with horrified certainty that it was about to take his head off.

From her perch outside, Jules grabbed his collar and yanked him out the window. The clang of the copper was louder than the alarm. It fell to the stone floor in a William Tell Overture–bashing, clanging, rolling, firework-accompanying smash.

"So much for a clean getaway," Jules said. They were on a narrow stone sill, high above the street. She gave a quick look below, then scanned the building above. "You said I'd never have to do this again. You *promised*."

"I don't think I promised, exactly," March said.

"What does 'I promise I'll never ask you to do this again' mean?"

"It means *I'm really hoping we never have to do this again*. And can we discuss this, you know, *below*?" March steadied himself against an iron railing that felt rickety.

Jules spoke into her headset. "D? We can't rappel down, all the lights are on. We've got to get to the roof. You see a way?"

Darius spoke, his voice urgent. "You went out the same way as the dude who broke in. He got up to the roof. Got to be a route. Look up."

"Genius, D." Jules scanned the roofline. "I see a hook."

"Okay, we're going to do some recon, see if there's a way to get you down in a safe spot. Those sirens are getting closer."

"Why is it always *up*?" March muttered.

"What kind of a jewel thief are you anyway?" Jules grimaced as she reached into her waist pack. "I can hook a carabiner onto the figure-eight descender and toss it up there. If I can hook around that baby, we're set. Of course, it'll be tricky," Jules said, lifting out the silks. "I can't test the hook. It could be rusted, or not able to hold the weight. And there's no swivel, so the silks might twist —"

March swallowed. "You're telling me that you don't know if the hook can hold us, but you're going to try anyway?"

"If I didn't set the hook, I don't trust it," Jules said impatiently. "But chances are it's good."

March felt his stomach twist. "I don't like *chances* when I'm a hundred feet above the pavement."

"Me neither, but it's our only shot. Unless you prefer prison."

"Hey, don't knock it. Three squares a day." March reflected that the joke would have come out better if his voice hadn't wobbled like a scaredy-cat.

Jules hesitated. "You can do this. You've been working on the silks for a year now."

She knew why he was so scared. March had seen his father fall off a roof. He'd heard the sound of him hitting stone. He'd seen the blood. Alfie had died holding his hand.

A roof was not March's favorite place to be.

"And we don't have options," Jules said. "What did Alfie say?"

"'If you don't have a choice, take it,'" March said.

Jules gauged the distance and tossed the carabiner. It landed on the hook. She tested the silk.

"I'll go first," Jules said. "If something goes wrong, better me than you."

"Wait. Why?"

Jules grinned. "Because I'm better in a crisis. Haven't you noticed?"

She climbed up the silk. March watched, his heart in his throat. The silk swayed, and Jules almost hit the building, but she made it to the roof and hooked one leg over the edge. In another moment she was safe above him.

She looked down at him, then motioned.

March heard the blare of a police siren, even louder now. *Wee-oh, wee-oh!*

It was either this or duck back in and get decapitated.

March chose the silk.

5

PLAN B

March started to climb. One hand at a time, the next grip, the next one after that. Jules had taught him well, but he still wasn't comfortable . . . dangling. His arm muscles shook with the effort.

Finally he was in reach of Jules's waiting hand.

"You gotta let go with one hand," she said.

"I can't."

"Look at me."

He looked into his twin's eyes. Their history together wasn't much. They'd been toddlers who shared a language. Then separated until they were almost thirteen.

Trust hadn't come easy for them. Now they had it.

He let go.

She grabbed him, hand to wrist, a C grip that she'd taught him a year ago as they hurtled through the darkness on a private plane, heading for another city, another heist. He hadn't known her that well then. Just well enough to know in his bones that she was his twin, that once she'd been as much a part of him as his own hand, his own arm.

He slid over the lip of the roof and landed on his face. March breathed in stone and metal and tar. He watched as a drop of sweat left his nose and pinged against the roof. He flipped over, drained.

Jules crouched next to him. "What's a cakewalk anyway?"

He groaned as he lifted himself up. "Not this."

Jules wrapped up the silk and stuffed it into her pack. She ran her hands through her short black hair. Sometimes he felt like he was looking in a mirror when he saw her. Pale skin, gray eyes, dark hair, thin face. But he guessed Jules was prettier. She was taller than he was, too, gaining two inches over him in one year. He tried not to mind.

March peered out over the city, the twisting streets and wide boulevards of Paris. He saw revolving red lights heading their way down the Boulevard Raspail.

Not good. He could feel panic surging up from the soles of his feet, but he fought it. Panic messed up your thinking process. He focused on the problem to keep his head clear. Just like Alfie would have.

"Darius? We need some help here."

"Okay, bro. You got to get to the north side of the roof. Next door to the gambling club. There's a parking lot — it's quiet. I think you can make the jump to the other roof."

"You *think*?"

"It's your best shot," Izzy broke in.

Jules moved across the roof ahead of him, sure-footed and quick. It was a typical Parisian roof, all different levels, with chimney pots to jump, skylights to avoid, gables to scramble down. They rolled, tumbled, leaped, and swerved across the obstacle course. Despite his nerves, exhilaration shot through March. Getaways were the best rush in the world.

Jules slid down a steep gable and landed on her feet. March followed, but suddenly he was on a slide going too fast, and straight down. Alarm stabbed him, and he grabbed frantically at an antenna, bending it almost to the roof as his heels scraped along the shingle.

Jules's hand shot out and saved him. She grunted as she pulled him to safety. March dusted the grit off his sweaty palms. "I totally had that, but thanks."

Darius stepped out of the shadow of a building below. It was hard to miss a six-foot-two fifteen-year-old with dreads to his shoulders. Izzy stood next to him, her curls tucked into a cap. She had just turned fourteen and barely came up to his shoulder. Izzy didn't talk much, but she had the tech brain of a geek and the heart of a lioness.

The police cars were closer now, moving fast on the empty street, their revolving lights flashing.

"Okay, we got this now," March said. "Time for Plan B. D and Iz, scatter."

"I'm not going anywhere until we know you're cool," Darius said. "Jump to the next roof, rappel down. We'll keep an eye out. If the police get here, hide in a car."

"He's right," Jules said, gauging the distance. "Let's get a running start."

March hesitated. "That's got to be a fifteen-foot jump."

"Nah. Fourteen and a half."

"Fifteen."

"Are we really going to quibble about six inches?" Jules asked, exasperated.

"Yes, if it's the six inches that mean I'm falling to my death!"

Jules grinned. "Together," she said. "One, two, three."

"Jump on three, or after three?"

"One . . . two —"

They ran flat out, then jumped into midair.

6

EMPTY POCKETS

They landed on the sloping roof, and each grabbed a corner of a gable. March hung on, sweating. Jules fastened two ropes, each one secure on a chimney. Or at least he hoped so.

"Toldja," Jules said. "Fourteen and a half."

They rappelled down the side of the building. March's hands were already sore, and he winced as he hit against the building and shot out again to rappel down.

He was grateful now that Jules had teased, bullied, and cajoled him into working out on the climbing wall they'd installed in the basement of their town house in New York City.

Home. As soon as he got back there, he would never leave again.

Jules was already halfway down, and he pushed off again, wincing as his ankle twisted. The rope slipped in his hands, he overcompensated, and the rope somehow wrapped around his ankle. He lurched sideways, then pitched forward, losing his balance completely. For one long second all he could see was the concrete of the parking lot below as his palms burned along the rope.

Then he gripped and yanked upward with all the strength he had. He stopped, upside down and swinging.

And then the worst thing happened, worse than falling — the sapphire dropped out of his pocket. Horror jolted him as it dropped like a lead weight, straight into the backseat of a

Mercedes convertible with its top down. March pulled himself straight, hit the wall, and plastered himself against it, cheek against stone. He had a secret pocket in his work clothes with a Velcro fastener. But for some reason he'd put the stone in his right pocket instead of his left. He'd never made a mistake like that before. Rusty.

"Push off again." Jules's voice was calm, but he heard the urgency. "You're almost there."

"The sapphire —"

"I saw it." Sirens screaming in his ears, March half fell, half rappelled down the remaining distance. He was never so glad to feel ground under the soles of his shoes.

He saw the stain of the red lights against the stone of the building as he ran toward the Mercedes.

"Stay put and find a place to hide," Darius said in his ear. "Cops have arrived. Iz and me fading back."

The alley door to the club started to open.

He didn't even have to look at Jules. They both jumped at the same time, vaulting over the door of the Mercedes and landing in the backseat. They hit the floor just as running footsteps headed toward them.

March and Jules leaned over, fingers frantically scrabbling along the carpet. It must have rolled under the front seat. March strained, his fingers splayed out, searching . . .

Almost got it . . .

Footsteps closer now . . .

There! His fingers closed around it.

The driver's-side door opened, and they heard the creak of upholstery. The door closed with a solid thunk. This was followed by the echo of the passenger door. *Thunk.*

Jules grabbed his hand, her eyes wide.

The engine turned over. March and Jules flattened

themselves like floor mats. He felt the surge as the Mercedes leaped forward.

They were trapped.

Still, was this so bad? They were escaping from the cops without even trying. The thought must have occurred to Jules at the same time, because she shrugged, then smiled.

The driver was driving like a careful old dude, easing around the corner.

March silently begged the dude to punch it, just a bit. The farther they got from the cops the better.

He heard the sound of a cell phone alert, just one quick chirp, and the driver answered it.

"Moving," he said in French.

Well, that was weird. Most people say hello.

Jules raised her head a bit to shoot him a quizzical look. March was concentrating on the flow of French.

He caught the word for diamonds . . .

And alarm . . .

He grabbed Jules's arm.

They were hiding in the getaway car!

7

RIVER VIEW

March couldn't pick up much from the rapid French, no matter how hard he tried. Random words fell into the back-seat like pebbles pelting him with stings of fear.

He translated the words in his head:

problem

stupid beast

imbecile

yes, we have diamonds

some gems missing

And the word he didn't want to hear:

kids

They'd been spotted.

Ask your protégé!

The phone must have winged across the seat, because March heard it clunk against the passenger door.

The sirens were suddenly loud and very close. A muttered curse rose from the driver's seat. The passenger still said nothing. The car leaped forward as the driver slammed on the gas.

The driver now made up for his earlier caution. March and Jules hung on to the carpet as the car squealed, turned, reversed, clattered down an alley (must be, the cobblestones rattling his bones), and made another quick turn.

The car squealed to a stop. The passenger door opened, then closed. Then the driver's door. *Thunk.*

March and Jules silently asked each other the question *what now?* They raised their heads cautiously. The car was parked at a corner, one of those corners in Paris where one street rose and another went down and another angled off. A figure in a black jacket and wool cap hugged the shadows, climbing the hill and disappearing. In the other direction a slender man in a suit was hurrying away, hands in his pockets, trying to look casual. He looked back once. And saw them.

"Oops," March said.

The man stopped. He stared, as though committing their faces to memory. He cocked his hand like a gun and aimed at them. Then he ducked down an alley.

March swallowed. "Did you see that?"

"Yeah." Jules sounded shaken.

Sirens screamed. A police car cut across three lanes of traffic and made a U-turn.

Jules clutched his arm. "They recognized the car! What do we do now?"

March vaulted into the front seat. "I'll drive."

"You don't know how to drive!" Jules cried as she scrambled into the passenger seat.

"How hard could it be?"

March put the car in gear, and it lurched forward, straight into a lamppost.

"Hard!" Jules yelled.

March searched for reverse. He backed up with a lurch, turned the wheel, and stepped on the gas.

If he didn't have to turn, he was okay. March raced along the boulevard. He suddenly realized where he was. He made a right that threw Jules against the door. "Sorry!" he yelled.

Now the river was to his left. Traffic was light at this time of night, which was a bonus. The Eiffel Tower was in his rearview and ahead he could see the dome of Les Invalides, where Napoleon was buried. He was in the 7th arrondissement, the posh district. If he could just stay straight on this road, he would be okay for a minute. He ran through his options. He could cross the river and try to lose them in the streets of the Pigalle. That would require driving skills he didn't have, however.

"Where are you going?" Jules screamed.

"I have no idea!"

"Okay, just get there faster!"

Where was the nearest metro station? He tried to remember, but he couldn't think, not when he was driving so fast. Then he remembered that the metro was closed. It was past three in the morning.

This wasn't good.

No matter how crazy the getaway, you've got to be clear.

Thanks, Pop. All I hear is static panic. Like somebody is screaming, and it's me.

Jules grabbed his arm. "Turn up there."

"Turn? Do I have to?"

"Yes!"

"Where?"

"There! Where the barrier is!"

"But there's a *barrier*!"

Jules reached over and yanked the wheel. Tires screamed, and March joined them. The car squealed into a hard left, crashing through a plastic gate and jolting down the stone pavers to the pedestrian walkway by the Seine. March's foot slammed on the brake. Only it was the gas.

The car hurtled toward the river as March's static panic turned into one long scream. Out loud.

8

A SORT-OF PLAN

Jules screamed, "NOOOOOOOOO!"

The car sideswiped a metal planter in a grouping filled with trees, teetered over the curb, and landed in the river in a burst of spray.

"OUT!" March yelled. He grabbed Jules and pushed her into action. She clambered over the seat in a frenzy, and he scrambled after her, over the backseat and sliding, heart slamming, over the trunk of the car as cold river water sluiced over the metal. Jules jumped, then crawled up the embankment, and landed on the stone pavers.

As the river soaked his pants, March felt something inside him shift. Some kind of dark veil dropped, and now he was *under* the river, unable to move, unable to breathe . . .

"MARCH!" Jules sobbed the word from the shore, holding her hands out in the air. "JUMP!"

March's brain clicked into reality. He was on top of a sinking Mercedes, which was beginning to tilt forward. He had less than a second. With a giant leap, he landed on the walkway, skidding against the cobblestones and tumbling forward, collapsing at Jules's feet.

March thought about kissing the ancient stones, but they looked pretty gross. They watched as eighty thousand dollars' worth of German engineering sank slowly in the Seine.

"We've got to get out of here," March said. "They'll double back."

Shivering, Jules jerked her head. "I know where I am. This way."

He trotted after her. Jules was moving fast, her eyes darting along the river. "I have a sort-of plan."

March stopped. Jules had fallen to her knees.

"Your plan is *praying*?"

"Help me!"

He dropped down. Jules's fingers yanked at a metal grate. "This is it, I'm sure of it."

He twined his fingers through the grate and pulled. With a soft thunk, it lifted, much easier than he'd imagined.

Jules shone her phone light. He saw the rungs of an iron ladder leading down.

"What —"

"Just. Go."

9

SWISS CHEESE

March climbed down the rungs as, above him, Jules resettled the grating. He felt carefully for each rung, then landed in a puddle. He could smell the river here, strong and green. Jules landed next to him and leaned against the ladder, breathing hard.

"That was a little too close," she said.

"You think?" March shivered. He felt like a drowned rat; he hoped he wasn't about to see one.

Just then the noise of a siren penetrated the gloom.

"Let's keep moving," Jules said.

"Right behind you."

Using her phone, Jules shone a light around the space until she located a square opening, barely big enough to squeeze through. She bent over and crawled into it. March followed.

He found himself in a narrow stone passage, its walls weeping with moisture. They splashed through puddles as they moved through it.

"It will be drier when we get away from the river," Jules said. "This tunnel floods."

March's socks were so wet it felt like he had sponges in his shoes. "How did you know about this place?"

"Been here before," Jules said shortly.

They walked farther down the passage and came to another ladder leading down.

"This is the main entrance," she said.

"Entrance to what?"

"The underground life of Paris. Below the city. Parisians call it *le gruyère* — you know, like Swiss cheese? Paris is built on a maze of tunnels."

"Like the catacombs."

"Yes, they're part of it, but these tunnels don't have bones."

"That's the most encouraging thing you've said so far."

"Limestone mines," Jules said, sending the light along the walls. "It's what Notre Dame and the Louvre were built with centuries ago. It created a whole vast network of tunnels. There's a whole society down here. Mostly young people who come for exploring, and parties and dances and picnics. There's even a movie theater carved out of the rock. Completely illegal, of course."

"Cool."

"There are rules, though. Whatever you bring down here, you take out. We can head to the exit near the Sorbonne. It's by the apartment."

"How do you know all this?"

Jules's face changed in that way that he knew she was about to bring up her past. "Blue did shows down here a few times. We set up a pitch in a place called La Plage — 'the beach.'"

Jules hardly ever mentioned the aunt who had raised her. Even the sound of her name was like some weird, mangled bell clanging doom. Blue had killed Alfie, pushed him off that rooftop. She'd raised Jules to be a street performer, just like her. She'd never loved her. March felt the familiar rush of heat, the need to punch a wall.

He was going to get Blue back someday for everything she'd done. But most of all for putting that blank, remote look in Jules's eyes. It scared him how sometimes Jules went away to a place he couldn't reach.

"Do you hear that music?" March asked quickly.

Jules turned and followed the sound of a guitar and a harmonica. They passed through a large room with a ledge thickened by wax from countless dripping candles, and a smaller passage with a colorful mural of a world on fire.

A young couple with a lantern and a string bag of groceries appeared out of a dark passage. They greeted Jules and March with a polite *salut* and brushed past them to enter a room off to the side. March glanced in and saw a dinner party in progress, glowing with lanterns and candles. Young people laughed around a stone table. Speakers connected to a phone softly played electronic music.

A few turns later the tunnel opened into a vast room. Young students sat around with bottles of wine and bread and cheese and sausage. In the corner a duo played a guitar and violin. A few couples were dancing, twirling gently in a small circle. Someone lifted a hand in welcome.

"Sorbonne?" Jules asked. She gestured with a finger, pointing up.

A slight, pretty girl in jeans and boots stood. "Americans! Have you been to Brooklyn? I am dying for Brooklyn." *Brook-leeen.*

"Sure," Jules said. "It's cool. But we need to get to the Sorbonne."

"I can tell you. If you follow the tunnel to the third turning, then go right at the blue graffiti, then left at the skull, you'll see a stairway leading up. It's a manhole, so you have to push, okay?" *Poosh.*

"Right at the graffiti, left at the skull," March muttered. "Do you think that's what the GPS would say?"

Just then a long-haired guy in an orange scarf ran into the space. "Catacops!"

The lounging students sprang up. Bottles of wine were corked and shoved into backpacks, food tossed into bags, candles snuffed out, music system dismantled and disappeared.

Within seconds, they were alone in the darkness.

10

LEFT AT THE SKULL

"Was that left at the skull or right at the skull?" March asked nervously.

Just then the young woman materialized next to Jules. "It's okay. Follow me."

They walked behind her in near-darkness through the tunnels, twisting and turning. "The cops come down sometimes," the girl said, introducing herself as Juliette. "But Rolf said there were a lot of them this time. Unusual."

They could hear noises of rushing footsteps, but it was impossible to tell which direction they were coming from.

"Don't worry, I know these tunnels better than anyone," she said. "You picked a good guide."

They walked for twenty minutes, staying close to Juliette. March's pulse skittered whenever he heard footsteps, but they only met other young people scattering to find the exits.

"Jean-Luc!" Juliette called to a young man who appeared in the tunnel ahead. She hurried toward him, and they greeted each other with kisses on both cheeks. Juliette exchanged a few words and then hurried back to them as Jean-Luc turned off the main tunnel. "Jean-Luc says it seems like they're looking for someone." She eyed them with sudden suspicion. "You are awfully young to be down here, you know? How old are you anyway?"

"Sixteen," Jules said promptly. "We did sneak out," she said with a short laugh. "But believe me, we're heading home. Are we almost there?"

Juliette chewed on her lip for a moment. Then she shrugged. "Almost. But let's move faster."

They picked up the pace, hurrying behind her and brushing past the weeping walls, the graffiti, the half-burned candles. Finally, Juliette stopped. "If you go up 'ere, you'll be near the church — Saint-Etienne-au-Mont. Just *poosh* 'ard on the manhole. I go on for a bit."

She gave them a little wave and walked on. They scrambled up the ladder. Carefully, they *pooshed* at the manhole and peered out. The street was empty. They crawled out and ran.

The safe house had been arranged for them. It was a small apartment in a building with an interior courtyard, mostly inhabited by students. The courtyard was full of cracked stones and weeds, with a small iron table and chairs. March and Jules ran up the stone stairs, their centers worn from thousands of footsteps over hundreds of years. The staircase wound around and around until it narrowed and they had to go single file to the top floor. As they approached the door, it opened, and Darius greeted them with a raised eyebrow.

"First trip to Paris, and so far, I don't even have a T-shirt." He tried to joke, but they could see the concern on his face. "Where *were* you? We tried to get you on the earpiece, but you must have been out of range."

"It's okay. The earpieces are in the Seine. With the car." March collapsed onto the couch. Suddenly, he could hardly keep his eyes open.

Izzy appeared like a ghost at Darius's side, her big brown eyes watchful. "Are you okay? We were scared."

"Nothing a week in Tahiti wouldn't cure."

She smiled, revealing the dimples you could practically crawl into.

"Did you get the loot?" Darius asked.

"No diamonds. We only got this," March said. He carefully put the star sapphire in the middle of the coffee table.

It was a trick of the moonlight, maybe, but the silver star suddenly flickered like a flame.

"Whoa," Darius said, taking a step forward.

"It's beautiful," Izzy said, taking a step back. "I don't like it."

A white curtain stirred, billowing out and molding, for the briefest of seconds, into a female form.

"Uh. Did anyone else . . . see that?" Darius swallowed. "Because I definitely didn't."

"A trick of the wind," Jules said.

"The window is shut," Izzy pointed out. Her eyes darted to the sapphire.

"You know these old French places." Jules slung an arm around Izzy. "Drafty. Voltaire probably lived here in, like, 1400 or something."

Izzy licked her lips. "Voltaire was born in 1694," she said. "And I'm getting a very strange vibe all of a sudden."

Jules smoothed Izzy's hair. She was more gentle with Izzy than with any other human. "Izzy, you don't believe in ghosts."

"Actually . . ."

Darius frowned. "You feeling something, Iz?"

"A . . . presence," Izzy said.

"What are you talking about?" March asked, rubbing his eyes.

"Izzy doesn't talk about it much, but she's what you call sensitive when it comes to spirits," Darius said. "Didn't we ever tell you about the ghost she saw on Spring Street?"

"Okay, cut it out," March said. "I've been spooked enough tonight."

"Maybe it's a friendly ghost," Jules said to Izzy.

Izzy didn't pick up on her light tone. "Spirits aren't friendly," she said. "They have a mission. Something holds them to life, but they can't grasp it. They haunt streets, or houses. Sometimes even objects." Izzy crossed her arms, hugging herself. "They're here to find something they lost, or to make something right. And sometimes they're here for revenge."

11

HOW HAMISH TALKED
THEM INTO IT

A month ago, back in New York, Hamish Tarscher, yogi, healing crystals expert, and crook, had asked March for help. "Foolproof heist. Easy money, easy in, easy out. Cakewalk!"

"No way," March had said. "I'm retired."

"If Einstein had retired, we wouldn't be on the moon!"

"I'm no Einstein."

"Sure, you are. If he'd been a crook. You have a *gift.*" Hamish handed him a glass of green juice, which smelled like grass and old dandelions.

Hamish ran an East Village shop that sold crystals and yoga mats, but his real work was as a fence. Bring Hamish a chunk of diamond, and he could cut it into five perfect solitaires — or sell it to the right person, who wouldn't ask too many questions. He'd been Alfie's best friend, and one of a tribe of "uncles" and "aunts" who had been a presence in March's life since he was a toddler, or at least when Hamish wasn't at the racetrack.

Hamish had leaned back, pushing his gray ponytail behind his shoulder. "All right, then, I'll tell you."

"I didn't ask!"

"Drink your kelp juice. It's a long story. Okay, okay, I'll shorten it. I have this new line of homeopathic oils, and the condo roof in Florida has to be replaced —"

March surreptitiously poured his kelp juice into a potted

plant. Why did adults think their problems were so fascinating?

"And I got myself into a spot of trouble," Hamish continued, rubbing his friendship bracelet. "There's this balloon payment — if my lovely wife finds out about it, she will leave me and move to Mexico — so I find myself with an urgent need for cash. I wouldn't ask you to do this if it wasn't a walk in the park. A strawberry smoothie on a summer morning! I promise you!"

"Never trust a sentence that starts with 'I promise you.'"

"Ah, Alfie, right? He's so right! But in this case, he's wrong!" Hamish chortled. "I have blueprints of the house. I know every single thing about the mark down to what he has for breakfast and when he last saw his urologist. The odds are in our favor. And I taught you odds at the racetrack when you were a mere boy." Hamish reared back and held up his hands. "Not that you should help me out for sentimental reasons! Oh no. This is strictly biz. I wouldn't want you to feel obliged, even though I was Alfie's BFF, and I'm your honorary uncle, and I've done you enormous favors."

March wasn't buying what Hamish was selling. No way. But Hamish *had* helped the gang, over and over — sometimes without even being paid. Even resourceful kids need an adult once in a while. They'd all run away from what they still called the Worst Group Home in the History of Child Care Services and landed in New York, looking for moonstones, and completely on their own. They'd lost the moonstones but found Alfie's legacy: a diamond as big as a walnut. The Makepeace Diamond had bought them everything they wanted — a real home. With twenty million dollars, they didn't have to worry about money ever again.

They only had to wish for something, and they would have it. That plus no school meant they basically lived in kid paradise.

But they still needed important adult things, like electricity. Things you needed a bank account for. Apparently even criminals had to pay taxes. Hamish had helped them with all that.

"Besides, young March, haven't you" — Hamish placed his hands together, his eyes twinkling — "missed the old life at *all*? Going straight is hard for us. I could never seem to manage it."

That's when March had known he was sunk. Because he *did* miss it. He missed the puzzle of figuring out how to get in and how to get out. He missed the clockwork exhilaration of a perfect plan. He still thrilled at the word *heist*.

So he'd said yes. And the rest of the gang had signed on. Even Jules, who had never liked thieving and was completely relieved to go straight. She'd prefer to dangle on her silks in a gym. Despite her great criminal skills, she was basically an honest person.

March didn't hold it against her.

After this harrowing night, after not even getting the diamonds, he still felt more alive than he'd felt in months. Besides, he got to do a favor for a friend.

Chump, Alfie said in his head. *I wouldn't have done it.*

12

THE GATE OF HEAVEN

After a fuzzy, distorted moment, Hamish appeared on the tablet. His ponytail was loose, and his wiry gray hair streamed to his shoulders. His wooden beads looked like they were strangling him.

"At last!" he said. "I'm on my third cup of green tea, I'm about to levitate! Is everybody okay?"

"We're all okay," March said. "Couple of things went wrong."

"NO! What?"

"One, the housekeeper came back from Brittany and called the cops."

Hamish groaned. "Always a problem in Paris, I'm telling you. Housekeepers! So unreliable! Minds of their own! Did she see you? Did you get the jewels? What's the second thing?" He put a hand on his chest. "Bad news first, so if I have a heart attack, at least I die knowing."

"Another thief broke in while we were there. They stole the diamonds."

Hamish got up from the chair, stamped his foot, and sat down again. "Who? I curse their karma!" he yelled.

"We're okay, thanks," March said. "I just had to drive into a river."

"Did you see who it was?"

"And I was almost decapitated."

"Decapitation?" Hamish leaned so close his face was distorted. "Fascinating! Uh . . . in what way, exactly?"

"Never mind. But we did manage to pick up this." March held up the sapphire.

Hamish let out a strangled cry of excitement. He straightened. "Can you rotate that stone, maybe shine a light on it?"

Jules aimed her cell flashlight while March held it up and turned it.

"It can't be," Hamish said, slamming both hands down on the table. The image jumped.

"What is it?"

"A shock to my already overloaded system, that's what!" Hamish cried. "I can't be sure, but . . . I'm not seeing it in person, but it could be . . . because it's so distinctive . . . the size . . . and that color . . . oh, I just saw the star! They're right! It's eerie!"

"What is it?" Jules asked.

"The Morning Star!" Hamish crowed. "I'm almost sure of it. Every gemologist knows about it. One of a trio of cushion-cut sapphires from Ceylon, set in a necklace for Anne Boleyn called the Gate of Heaven. The stones have been missing for, oh, fifteen years or so. They're known for their color, purity, and the . . . shall we say *otherworldliness* of the star at the heart of each of them. The necklace was also owned by Marie Antoinette."

"Whoa, two headless queens," Darius observed.

"Decapitation seems to be a theme here," March said. He remembered the spinning heavy metal tray and wondered. *Could it have? Really?*

"Rather well and gruesomely put," Hamish said.

"Hamish, is this stone enough to get you out of trouble?" Jules asked.

"Here is the thing, young yogis," Hamish said. "Sometimes things happen in Adult World. Let's call it a poopshow. In other words, everything goes wrong at once. That appears to have happened to your fine fellow here. So, in a word? Close but no cigar. Individually, the stones are too hard to move. Too recognizable with that red flash. I'd have to cut them into smaller gems. Hardly worth it. However, all is not lost!"

All is never quite lost with Hamish, March thought. *There is always another angle.*

Hamish stood. "We are *this* close —"

"Ham, we can't see you, man," Darius said. "How close is *this* close?"

Hamish sat down again. He held up his thumb and index finger. "This close! To achieving the greatest challenge in history!"

"What?" Jules asked.

"Well, jewel thief history," Hamish said. "Which is the best kind of history, let's face it." He clasped his hands. "What if we were able to reunite them?"

13

MY DAD IS A NAG

"Think about it," Hamish said. "If I were to locate the *other two* sapphires, and you were to steal them in the same brilliant fashion, then, well, we'd have a fortune beyond our wildest dreams. Alone, you just have three sapphires worth not much. Reunite the three . . . you could buy a private island! A castle in Spain! And I could settle a few enormous debts I have outstanding."

"I don't want a castle," Izzy said. "And we're already rich."

"We were in for one heist to help you out. Not three," March said.

"I realize that, but if you are sitting on a beach fishing and a wonderful starfish falls into your lap, do you throw it back?"

"Yes!" March cried.

"Bad example. If you buy one lottery ticket, but the game is fixed and you know the *next* ticket would net you a hundred million dollars, do you just pay for your one scratch-off five-dollar ticket and your pomegranate juice and *leave*?"

March pretended to knock his head against the table.

"You're on a video feed. I can see what you're doing," Hamish said. "My point being. There are undoubtedly certain parties who would in fact pay a tremendous amount to reunite these stones. Maybe even remake the Gate of Heaven. There's some rich dame out there who wants Marie Antoinette's necklace, you can bet on it. Thirty, forty, fifty million — who knows? All it takes is a bit of research, some nefarious contacts — both of which I am good at — and then planning, to which I tip my hat to the mastermind, March McQuin, the worthy successor to his noble father — *don't shut off the computer* — my dearest pal, Alfie, plus the stealthiest, smartest gang of thieves on the planet."

March looked at the others. Jules was frowning, Darius looked uneasy, and Izzy eyed the sapphire with something close to fear.

As for him, his blood was racing.

"Look, I was in this for one job," Jules said. "I *like* being retired."

"This was a close one, Ham," Darius said. "We've got one gem. We're already sitting on a fortune. I've invested it wisely in tax-sheltered accounts with high-yield securities."

"I have no idea what that means," Izzy said. "But thanks."

"In other words, we have enough for ten lifetimes," Darius said. "Love you, man, but I'd rather just chill on my pile of cash."

"I don't like that sapphire," Izzy said.

March knew they were right. He felt everything they felt. So what if he *also* felt a sharp pang at the thought of missing out on the Gate of Heaven?

It's a lifetime score, kid. Only comes around once. Who doesn't want thirty, forty, fifty million? Plus, you know, jewel thief history. You'd be up there with your old man. You and me, kid, legends in our own time.

March tried to ignore Alfie. His dad was a nag. "Sorry, Ham. We're —"

"Now, don't rush to answer yet —"

"— not interested."

Hamish's long, mournful face got even longer, even sadder. "Oh. Well. Far be it for me to question why the son of

Alfie McQuin would turn down the chance to make jewel thief history, but what can you do?" He brightened. "I have an idea! You deserve a vacation. Why don't you come to Miami? I'm at my condo. The sunshine is sublime."

"No, just get us out of here," March said. "Last night was too close. Can we get an earlier flight?"

"I live to serve. I'll text you the deets."

They said good-bye, and March closed the computer.

"He's not going to give up," Darius said.

March stretched. "I know."

"Sunrise in an hour," Jules said, crossing to the window.

March dived into the sofa and curled around a pillow. He remembered back to another almost-dawn, just like this one. The sky had been this same dark blue, his heartbeat had been jumping like this, and he'd been filled with a grief so huge he was afraid it was crushing him so hard he'd never walk again. He'd seen his father fall from a roof, had knelt by him on the cold, hard stones, and had seen the instant life left his body, and he had never felt so alone. The earth had seemed so wide and empty, and yet it had no place for him.

Now he had a place. He had family. He had Jules. He had Darius and Izzy, a tight group around him, all of them standing back-to-back against the world. He often pictured them that way, in a tight circle, faces out, ready for anything. It was a comforting way to fall asleep. He had his people, shoulder to shoulder. He had a place in the world.

He jolted awake when Darius said, "It's made the news."

Sunlight now streamed through the window. Darius held the tablet in front of March's face. Under a blurry sense of headlines (TALKS CONTINUE/IMPACT REPORT/FRENCH REFUSE/ AMERICANS INSIST . . .), one smaller headline popped out:

ROBBERY AT INDUSTRIALIST'S PARIS MANSION
Police Suspect Organized Gang
Housekeeper Insists Kids Were Culprits
March groaned and put his hands over his face.
"We're made," Darius said.

14

BREAKFAST IN PARIS

Izzy sat in front of the laptop. "No video, no pictures of us," she said. "That's good."

Darius sat down close to March. "Hey, Marcello. Do they have food in Paris?"

"Is that a hint, Mr. D?"

"Nah. Just an idle inquiry. From someone who could basically eat a bear right now. And I'm a vegetarian."

"You're not a vegetarian."

"Well, except for pepperoni. Even vegans don't expect you to give up pepperoni."

"Don't try to figure it out," Izzy said. "Just feed it."

Darius tossed a pillow at her, and she stuck out her tongue. Darius and Izzy had the longest history of the gang. Darius had watched over Izzy since she was a tiny nine-year-old who'd arrived in the group home straight out of a psych ward, where they'd put her after she had been left in a locked bathroom by her parents while they went off to Atlantic City to gamble. They'd left her with food for two days. They were gone for five.

"I don't think we should all go out," March said. "I'll grab some food and be right back. In the meantime, pack the gear. Hamish got us on the noon flight. We can take the RER train to the airport."

The streets were full of morning commuters, heading to or from the metro, stopping for a quick espresso, riding bicycles in traffic, walking dogs and kids, doing all the things

French people do while looking amazingly nonchalant and cool. There was nothing like a day in early September in Paris to make you feel that the world was a lovely, busy, well-groomed place. March tried not to look too American. It was ridiculous how you could instantly spot an American in Paris. Baggy pants, fleece pullovers, running shoes. He passed an ambling middle-aged guy in a University of Michigan T-shirt. They might as well carry a sign saying PICKPOCKETS CHOOSE ME.

He remembered enough of his time in Paris to know where the farmers' markets — *les marchés* — were, and on what days. Alfie preferred to shop in open-air markets in Paris rather than the local bakeries and greengrocers, where a face might be remembered.

Paris had been their favorite city. He and Alfie had stayed here in flush times and lean times, and it was always fun. He climbed the gentle hill behind the apartment and made his way through Saint-Germain. March cruised by the offerings, picking up fruit, cheese, a dried sausage, and some pastries. He bought more than he needed and told the stall owners to keep the change. Scrounging was a thing of the past. He left the *marché* and stopped at a *boulangerie* for baguettes. The yeasty, warm loaves were too tempting, and he tore off the top of one to munch on the way back to the safe house.

It was amazing to think that last night he'd been under all this sunlit *busyness*, in candlelit caverns and twisting corridors carved out of ancient rock.

He wasn't sure when he had become aware, but suddenly he knew he was being watched. Something had triggered it, some sixth sense he'd developed growing up with Alfie. It was as though a shadow cast from nothing suddenly hit the back of his neck. March knew better than to turn. He glanced in a shop window.

The guy in the University of Michigan T-shirt was behind him now. The same guy he'd seen near the market.

Coincidence?

If Coincidence shows up, Trouble follows.

TOP CATS

"Hello, March."

The guy looked like just another American tourist in Dad jeans. Except . . . not.

How to ID a cop: Just look at the eyes.

Thanks, Pop. I've got this. The guy's a cop.

"Saul Dukey, FBI."

Not just a cop — a fed! March's gaze moved fast, searching out the exit options. No metro station nearby, and if he ran, the street was wide and straight. But the Boulevard Saint-Michel was only about five blocks away, and he could lose himself in the students . . .

"Relax, kid. Nowhere to run. Let's have a chat."

It was the way he said it. With authority that didn't have to push. March knew it would be a mistake to run.

And, looking at him, March knew it would do no good to pretend he wasn't March McQuin. This guy knew exactly who he was. "You're out of your jurisdiction," he said. "The FBI can only operate in the United States."

"Not really. Interpol called us in. I'm an invited guest." He studied March for a moment that felt longer. "I was a friend of your dad's."

"Yeah, I remember all those heartwarming family dinners we had with you."

Dukey gave a half smile. "You remind me of him."

"Must be the chin."

"No, it's the *mouth*, actually. Look, I owe him a favor."

"I've got news for you. It's a little late."

"What I'm saying is I'm passing it along to you. The favor." He tilted his head. "Let's walk, all right? Paris is a great city for walking. So they say."

Like he had a choice. March tried to unobtrusively look around. Were there more agents hovering, ready to pounce?

"Relax, it's just us. This time." Dukey looked over March's bag and selected an apple. He polished it on his shirt. "Ever hear of the Top Cat gang?"

"Who hasn't?" They were the most nefarious jewel thief gang in Europe. Known for their daring and style, they pulled off heists in broad daylight. Their escape methods were legendary — a speedboat in Cannes, a helicopter in Zurich, the Underground in London. They had dressed up as women and bank officials and rich clients. They would go anywhere and steal anything. There were dozens of members, maybe more, a whole network of larceny that crisscrossed Europe and Asia. They took their name from an old television cartoon about a tribe of thieving street-smart alley cats.

"French police got a tip that they're targeting the States. Setting it up for a full-scale invasion of the gang. So I came over here to share information with Interpol. Being the jewel thief expert and all." He took a bite of the apple.

"Not sure what this has to do with me," March said.

"We hear that they have an American associate. I've been looking for that contact for months."

"Yeah, it might net you a big promotion, right?"

"It would make my career, sure, but who cares," Dukey said, his eyes flickering briefly. "But let me tell you about this weird coincidence. So I'm here, meeting with the officers assigned to track the Top Cats, and what do you know, they pull off a heist last night! There I was, right on the front lines."

March's pulse ticked. He moved the bag to the other side and squeezed it tight. Dukey chewed and swallowed. "Typical heist. The housekeeper is pretty hysterical. Came home early, caught them in the act. The rich French guy is groggy — said he'd taken a sleeping pill. One thing is funny, though. The housekeeper says the thieves were kids. Can you imagine that?"

"You said she was hysterical."

"Stuck to the story, though. She said they did some major acrobatics on these crazy pipes they have in the place. And the investigators who know everything there is to know about the gang? They say she must be mistaken — kids don't work for the gang. Interesting tidbit, am I right?"

"Bewitching," March said. "But —"

Dukey held up a hand. "Wait and see where I'm going with this, 'cause it's a great story. We get a message that the police are in the middle of a high-speed chase. We got the coordinates, so we take off, take a couple of short-cuts, wind up near the river."

"They call it the Seine."

"You don't say. So the getaway car is this big old convertible Mercedes, interesting choice, but come to think of it, Top Cat style. We hear that the gang's best wheelman was spotted at the wheel, only now it's driving like a crazy person, weaving all over the place. It crashes through a barricade and dunks in the river. We're pulling up, okay? I'm looking down that walkway by the river. And I could swear I see a couple of kids. Running. So what do I do? I take off after them. I lose them for a sec, and they just . . . disappear. What do you think about that?"

"I think you owe me a euro for that apple."

"Hang on, it gets better. One of the cops tells me that we're near an entrance to these tunnels below Paris. I say, 'You're kidding me,' and they say, 'Hey, let's check it out pronto.' Or however you say that in French. So I spend about an hour down there in these tunnels, and let me tell you, it's amazing. Quite a scene down there. Kids everywhere, but suddenly, there was some kind of signal, because . . . *poof!* They disappear! So we all give up."

March felt relief flood him. Dukey had nothing after all. He was just fishing.

Dukey waved the apple. "And that's when I meet Juliette."

Hooked.

16

THIEVES GET CAUGHT

March swallowed. He tried not to show his panic. *Never let them know they've got you.* "So it's a love story. Aw. Congratulations."

He pointed the apple at March. "Happily married man, son. No. She's hanging out by the entrance, gets freaked by the cops, but she calms down when I tell her I'm looking for a couple of kids. Turns out she walked them to an exit and was worried. They seemed kinda young. So I ask her what exit, and she brings me there. And so this morning I hang around — these French cafés are great for that, by the way — and what do you know, I see Alfie's kid March. As they say in France, *quel* surprise-o."

"So you're fluent in French," March said. *"Mais ce n'était moi."*

"So you can lie in French, too."

Dukey's gaze had turned hard. March felt a sudden lurch in his stomach. His mouth went so dry he couldn't have spit if he'd wanted to.

"Funny how you're here at the same time as when a big heist goes down," Dukey continued. "You're in a tunnel at four o'clock in the morning."

"Agent Dukey, I'm not in the family business."

"Seems to me you were mixed up in a moonstone caper last year. Ten million dollars in bonds went missing."

"I hadn't heard about it," March said. In his head, Alfie said, *Never admit anything.*

"I know you didn't steal them. I understand your aunt was involved. Becky Barnes, also known as Blue."

"We're not close."

Dukey snorted. "Good call. I've been trying to get the goods on her for fifteen years." He tossed his apple in the trash. "You want to talk to me about last night?"

"Did some sightseeing, went to bed early."

"You want to rethink that answer?"

"No. You don't have anything," March said, returning the man's stare.

Dukey sighed and looked off for a second. "The only reason we're having this conversation is because your old man was a stand-up guy — for a crook. He saved my life a couple of years ago. And he didn't have to. I was undercover, the deal went down, and suddenly everything went south. If it wasn't for Alfie McQuin, I'd be at the bottom of the Thames River." He raised an eyebrow. "That's in London."

"Who knew?" March felt a memory kick to life. He was eleven. He was waiting in a hotel in Calais for Alfie to return from London on a big caper. Alfie didn't show up for three days, and then they jumped on a train and went to Spain. Now he remembered Alfie's nerves, how he didn't relax until they crossed the border. *Busted, bud*, Alfie had said. *Back to living thin.*

"Cost him a cool million. Had to give up his share to save me. So, I owe him. Otherwise you and your little gang of four would be back on a plane, headed for juvenile hall, but not until you'd been thoroughly questioned by the French police, Interpol, and the FBI."

The panic he'd managed to tamp down was now banging on every nerve.

How does he know we're four?

"Yeah, I know who's in the gang. Apparently you're not as good as you think you are at hiding out."

Is he bluffing? March wondered. *How could he have found us?*

"I had a notion you'd turn up at Alfie's grave sooner or later."

March's heart fell. He knew it had been risky. It had been only a few months ago, the anniversary of Alfie's death, and he just couldn't help himself. They had all gone, taking the train upstate and leaving some of Alfie's favorite things — black licorice, a bottle of cream soda, a John Scofield jazz CD — on his grave. Stupid.

They catch you on sentiment, kid. Wall it off.

He wanted to kick himself. How many times had Alfie told him not to look back? *If we could do a 180, we'd be owls.*

"Cemetery owner tipped me off. I had local cops follow you to the train. Gave me enough time to get to Grand Central, but you never showed up."

Because they'd gotten off the train in Harlem and taken the subway. Darius had been hungry for pizza.

"It was easy to track back and find out where you and your sister, Julia, were assigned. A couple of really heart-warming types named Pete and Mandy Sue clued me in that you disappeared with two of the kids there — Darius Fray and Isabel Mercado. Mercado's parents are rumored to be hackers operating in Argentina — when they're not gam-bling in Macao — and Fray's mother has a rap sheet as long as my arm, currently out on parole. Nice group you run with."

Made. All of them. March tried to keep his face neutral, but his pulse was skittering. How could he have missed that tail? Small-town cops from dinky Fortune Falls, following them to the train?

Because he'd gotten lazy. Because he'd been dazed and sad from standing over Alfie's grave.

Because he missed his dad everywhere — in the streets of Paris, in the home Alfie had made for him and never told him about, every time he ate a piece of licorice or checked the Yankees score. Every time he opened his eyes in the morning.

"Funny how the Top Cat heists started right about when you dropped off the radar. This past year was a busy one — jobs in Milan, Dubrovnik, Copenhagen . . . that was an interesting one. They ran a line from one building to another, seemed to have swung in a half-open window . . . skills your sister has. She was a street performer, right?"

"She's retired."

"Uh-huh." Dukey stepped in front of March. March had to stop short so he wouldn't slam into him. His gaze was like a concrete wall.

"If you think running with this gang is fun, you're wrong. They are vicious, hardened criminals. If you can ID them, you're dead. They'll use you and they'll throw you away, and they won't particularly care if you're dead when they do it."

"I'm not a Top Cat!"

Dukey raised his eyebrows. "Then you're in bigger trouble. You got in their way. Not to mention their getaway car. They'll be looking for you."

"I doubt it, since I wasn't there."

"When they find you — and they will — they won't be nice about saying hello."

"Look, I got the message, okay?"

Dukey let out a sigh and looked away for a minute, scanning the street. "Let me tell you something, son. You got a raw deal, no question. Your old man wasn't bad, he was just good at the wrong things."

March swallowed against the rush of emotion that closed his throat. He hated it when people were nice about his dad. It made it worse, somehow, having to hear it.

"No reason you have to follow in his footsteps, though." He held up a hand. "I know, you're not. Right. Group homes are lousy, but the system is a picnic compared to this gang. My advice? Go back home, take a trip to Child Protective Services. You're what, fourteen now? You don't belong on your own."

"I'm not on my own," March said. "And don't call me son."

"Yeah, you have a posse. Wake up. You're *kids.* There are only two endings: jail or dead. Thieves always get caught. Because of guys like me." He leaned closer and grabbed March's wrist, closing his hand around it like a handcuff. "Snap," he said. Now he looked hard and mean. His gray eyes glittered, chips of fractured ice.

March shook off the hand, hard. "Thanks for the advice."

Dukey shrugged. "This meeting was payback. Now we're square. The next time I see you, I'll be bringing handcuffs."

17

FINISHED

Busted.

It was all his fault. He'd made a stupid amateur mistake, a mistake out of sentiment, just wanting to be near what was left of his dad. It was all so stupid. Alfie was ash and bits of bone in some ground under a stone marker. March hadn't found peace there. He hadn't found *closure*.

Jules, Darius, and Izzy had gone with him without even asking. They didn't want him to be alone. And because of that, they were busted, too. How could he tell them?

His fault.

When he walked back into the apartment, they all charged toward him.

"Food!" Darius said, grabbing the bag. "You took your time, Marcello. Hey, you ate my bread!"

They moved into the kitchen. Jules began to slice the rest of the bread. Izzy pulled fruit and cheese from the bag. Darius found plates. March watched as the three worked together, handing one another plates and glasses, moving around one another, tossing an apple, giving a taste of the cheese . . . a dance. They knew one another's moves.

Routine. Habit. Trust. Knowing the person will be there to catch the apple before you toss it.

He'd blown it.

Darius offered his apple, and Izzy took a bite. Jules finished slicing the cheese and arranged the slices like the rays of a sun.

He couldn't tell them.

Not yet.

At Charles de Gaulle Airport, they passed through security and walked toward the gate. The botched heist and the lack of sleep created a fog they couldn't break through.

Jules leaned her head closer to March. "Up ahead, at three o'clock, I got a guy."

The guy was sipping on a cup of coffee. His eyes were scanning the passengers in an idle way, his mouth twisted slightly as he tracked the rolling suitcases and bags full of last-minute purchases of French perfume and mustard. Watching. Too intently. While trying not to look like it.

Cop. Could be for them. Could be not. Didn't matter. Evasive action.

March slowed his steps. "We've got to split up. Follow the plan."

It was a drill they had gone over already, practiced just in case of trouble.

Izzy back.

Jules left.

March right.

Darius way back.

Without exchanging another word, they melted into the crowd, Izzy fading back, Jules heading for the restroom behind them, Darius making a 180 and heading back toward the duty-free shops.

March stopped at the water fountain near the restrooms. With his head bent, he scanned the hallway. It took only thirty seconds or so before an American family straggled by, led by an impatient dad rolling a stuffed carry-on, then a mom with a shopping bag and a young kid, while directly behind them trudged a bored teen in headphones . . .

March fell into almost-step with the teen girl.

"Heading home?"

She took out one earbud and gave him a look as though he were too young and nerdy to dare talk to her. "Well, duh."

"I'm heading to Chicago." He waved a finger at her screen. "I like your playlist."

She snatched her phone closer. "Bug off, dweeb."

"That's *le dweeb*, actually," March said.

But they were past the guy now, and his gaze was sweeping the corridor behind March. They'd looked like two squabbling siblings, he knew.

Now he just had to hope the rest of the crew would make it through. If the guy was a cop. Or worse, FBI.

If you have a bad feeling about something, you're usually right.

Not very reassuring, Pop.

You want reassurance or you want real?

The rest of the gang showed up as they called the flight, just as planned. They got to board early as unaccompanied minors. They were sprinkled around the plane. March immediately plugged in his headphones and grabbed a blanket.

He was desperate to sink into a deep, dreamless sleep, but his mind didn't stop pinging crazily from Dukey saying *there are only two endings* and the Mercedes sliding into the cold river.

The worst part of a close call was after.

His knees were up to his chin, his seat didn't recline, and he couldn't get a flight attendant to get him a glass of water.

He'd been in tough situations with Alfie. Jobs had gone wrong; police had dragnets. Alfie had been double-crossed once or twice. March wasn't completely busted — they didn't know where he lived. But he was uncomfortably aware that he hadn't set aside what Alfie called "walking-away money." Something to access if home wasn't safe and they needed to bolt. That would be item number one on his to-do list when he got back.

Finally he dropped into a deep sleep.

He didn't wake up until the pilot announced that they were landing in thirty minutes. He saw Jules emerge from the bathroom. As she passed him, she tossed a piece of paper in his lap.

The guy is on the flight. Seat 35C.

18

SCHOOL'S OUT

March met Jules by the bathrooms.

"So who is it?" she asked. "French police? Do you think we'll have cops at the gate?"

"It might not be for us," March said.

"We can't take that chance! What I don't get is, how did they track us so fast?"

March shifted his feet. "It's not the cops. It's the FBI. I think."

"What?"

A flight attendant looked over, and March smiled at her and pointed to the bathroom. "Look, I didn't tell you something," he confessed to Jules. He quickly explained about Agent Dukey and his warning.

Jules dug her hands in her pockets. "Are you kidding me? The *feds* are onto us? And when were you going to part with this information?"

"I thought I'd wait until we were back home. But first we have to shake the tail."

"On a plane? What would you like to do, flush ourselves down the toilets?"

"Not helpful. Plus, gross."

The flight attendant came by and leaned in. "Sorry, kids. The captain has put on the seat belt sign. We'll be landing in a few minutes."

"Of course!" Jules said, and then didn't budge.

March looked at his phone. The airport would be crowded, but he couldn't count on losing the tail when they'd all be herded through customs. It would have to be after that.

If you're cornered, get invisible.

"New York City schools are back in session, right?" he asked Jules.

"Yeah. I can't wait to see who I get for biology."

"Forget the cab. We're taking the subway home."

Slowly, Jules grinned. "Perfect."

The New York City subway system was old, cranky, and occasionally filthy, but it was fast. It brought commuters and tourists and New Yorkers to their destinations with a rattling, jolting efficiency. With the exception of rush hours, you could usually find a seat, and the cars were quiet.

Except when school let out.

Then students from every borough flooded the system, high school and middle school and elementary school kids with parents in tow. By the time March and the gang made it onto the F train, it was packed with students. Not only students, but students at the end of the long school day who still missed summer vacation. They jostled, they hooted with laughter, they kidded, they studied, they stamped, they joked, they teased.

Quickly the gang split up and melted into the crowd. Darius moved to the next car, and March just kept moving down the subway car. He could feel the agent behind him, having a hard time making it through the small clumps of jostling students.

At Forty-Second Street the gang jumped off. It was a big station with lots of platforms. They ran for the downtown train. At the last moment March saw the agent just make it onto the train. Again they were swept up in the weaving, bobbing, hooting students.

The platform at the next station was packed. March and the gang exited the train and dived into the middle of the students. When the train arrived, they moved in a huge mass toward the doors. March could sense the man behind him, pushing through the crowd, keeping them in sight. They squeezed onto the train, staying near the doors. March saw the man push his way through the doors farther down. March and the gang stepped off. The agent stepped off. Not good.

"Express," March said.

The train across the track stopped, and people shuffled out. The platform was suddenly crowded again. The agent lost sight of them as students streamed up the stairs or waited for the local. At the last possible moment, March and the others jumped onto the express. The doors snapped shut.

As the train moved down the track, he saw the agent searching through the crowd, looking for them.

At Fourteenth Street they changed trains again. By the time they got to Franklin Street they were sure they hadn't been followed.

It was their stop. March walked down the familiar street, past the bakery, past the diner, past the bar that smelled like old beer. He was glad to be home.

"What's that?" Izzy asked as they came up to their building. On the front door was a large gray box, a lock that hooked through the door pull.

"It's a lock box," Jules said. "The kind a realtor puts on a door when a house is being sold."

They examined the box. They tried their key. The door wouldn't budge.

"What's going on?" Izzy asked in a small voice. Her dark eyes were anxious.

"This is weird," Jules said.

"This way," March said.

The alley gate was locked, and the combination didn't work. They exchanged worried glances and climbed over it. Another gray box secured the side door. March didn't even give it a look. He jumped up on the garbage can, a large, double-wide variety that easily took his weight. Now he was facing a small barred window. He took a small key from his inner pocket and lifted a metal shaving, revealing a small lock. He opened it, and the bars slid up into the window frame.

"Just in case we ever got locked out," he said to the others. "After you."

Jules crawled through the window, followed by Izzy. Darius put one leg in but couldn't fold himself inside. He tried going headfirst, but his shoulders got stuck.

"Not happening, bro," he said.

"I'll let you in the garage," March told him. He squeezed through the window opening.

They were in the gray cement hallway that led to the parking garage. March went inside and put in the combination to open the door. It rolled open, and Darius strolled inside.

They opened the maroon fire door and climbed the stairs to the first level.

Alfie had left March and Jules the penthouse apartment, but after their big score, they knew too many questions might be asked by the other tenants or the doormen, like *Where's your parent or guardian?* Or, eyeing two white kids, an African American, and a Puerto-Rican American, *Are you kids related?* So, with Hamish's help, they'd bought the whole building. They had left the first floor intact, and it still looked like a lobby in a luxury condo building. March tried the light, and it snapped on. He didn't know why he felt so relieved. He had a ticking sense of foreboding as he pushed the Up button on the elevator.

They'd done some basic renovations to the top floor, which became their hangout space — kitchen, media room, terrace, game room, and one room they used for storing all the stuff they'd bought and never used, like lacrosse sticks and polo mallets (a brief infatuation of Darius's) and the virtual reality helmets that never worked right. The floor below was their bedrooms. On the other floors they'd put in a lap pool and a gaming room and a trapeze. The garden was on the roof.

They took the elevator to the top floor, and it opened directly into the hangout area.

Izzy gave a small cry and grabbed Darius's arm. March and Jules stood stock-still, their mouths open.

It was empty.

19

CLEANED OUT

The four double-wide sofas, the long table where they ate and played computer games, the computer console, the sixty-five-inch flat-screen TV with surround sound. Gone. Wires twisted out of walls like hungry snakes. A plant gasped for water. An empty juice bottle lay abandoned in the corner.

"Wh-what happened?" Izzy asked.

"We've been robbed!" March said, kicking the juice bottle. "Cleaned out."

Izzy revolved in a slow circle. "It's like we were never here. Like it was a dream we dreamed."

Jules ran toward the spiral staircase that led to the floor below. A moment later they heard her shout. "My stuff is gone!" she yelled. "Everything! My books! My clothes! My paints! Everything's gone!"

March couldn't make sense of this. How could thieves come in and just take everything? He didn't want to look at his room. Didn't want to see the dust on the floorboards, the empty shelves.

Darius slid down the wall and put his head in his hands.

March felt for his phone. He'd forgotten to turn it on again after they exited the plane. He had seventeen texts from Hamish. They all said the same thing: *CALL ME*.

"Izzy! Get the tablet. We need to talk to Hamish!"

Hamish answered the call right away. Izzy set up her screen on the kitchen counter, and they all crowded around.

"There you are!" Hamish sat on the deck at his condo. It appeared that a palm tree was growing out of his head. "Or should I say, where are you?"

"We're at the house!" Jules broke in breathlessly. "It's been cleaned out!"

"Hmm. Yes. I have some, ah, lamentable news. Take a cleansing breath."

"We don't have time to breathe. We have a crisis here!" Jules sputtered. "We've been robbed! What are we supposed to do? Call the police?"

"Let's not get crazy. You weren't robbed," Hamish said. "I found out when I changed your plane reservations. Your debit card was canceled. There's nothing in your bank account. Checking or savings."

"Impossible!" March exclaimed.

"Ridiculous!" Jules yelled.

"Sometimes the ridiculous becomes a very dark reality. Just look at the House of Representatives."

"What about the house?" March asked. "How could we lose the house?"

"Apparently it's been sold."

"But how could that happen if we weren't here to sign papers?"

Hamish wrung his hands. "Because apparently all your assets were in a non-revocable trust."

Darius took a step back.

"What does that mean?" Izzy asked.

Darius reached for his phone. "You're wrong. Something else is happening. I'll ask Dougie."

"Who's Dougie?" Izzy asked.

"Our financial advisor," Darius said.

"We have a financial advisor named *Dougie*?" Jules asked.

"Remember I said that our money had to make money?" Darius asked. "That's the way the one percent keeps getting richer? And remember we took a vote, and you all voted to hire him?"

Hamish tilted his head. "His name wouldn't be Douglas Parmenter, would it?"

"Yes!" Darius said. "Brilliant dude. He manages the money of a whole bunch of celebrities."

"And he was the principal owner of the trust?"

"No, he *managed* it."

"No," Hamish said gently. "He was a principal trustee with the full authority to dissolve it. I'm sorry."

Darius looked lost. "Wait a second. You have the wrong guy. Parmenter graduated from Harvard Business School."

"Uh, not exactly," Hamish said. "Douglas Parmenter is a high school dropout from Grover Cleveland High in Queens. He collected aliases instead of degrees. Aka Dougie Paternicus, aka Richard Worthington, aka Richie the Rich, aka Rick the Flick —"

March felt a cavern of fear open up inside him. He almost didn't have to hear the rest. But he asked anyway. "You mean everything is gone? What about the yacht?"

"I'm afraid it just . . ." Hamish trailed a hand in the air. "Sailed away."

20

THE BIG STORE

Darius began to roam the space, shaking his head. "There's gotta be a mistake here," he said. "It can't be the same guy! Maybe he pulled the funds for investment. I'll just text him." Darius started working on his phone.

March turned toward Darius slowly, as though every muscle in his body ached. It felt that way, like he'd been beaten up. "How did you meet this guy?"

"At the bank," Darius said. "Totally legit. It was that time we needed to withdraw the cash for the climbing wall. We struck up a conversation. He looked like a banker, all fine in an expensive navy suit. Handmade shoes. He gets 'em in London."

"He overheard you with the teller," March said, rubbing his forehead. "We withdrew a bunch of cash that day. You were a mark. A pigeon."

"No way! I'm not stupid. I didn't just hand over my wallet!"

"Not right *then*, sure!" March roared. "You waited until you could hand over everything we had!"

Jules put her hands on her cheeks. "I can't believe this."

Darius swallowed. His voice shook as he said, "We just had a conversation. He said he worked for an investment firm. Gave me his card. I even went to his office. Some swanky place downtown. He had a gorgeous secretary and a huge desk —"

March sank to the floor. "The Big Store."

The Big Store was a famous con. The con man just rented an empty office, or an apartment, or whatever he or she needed, then window-dressed it to impress clients. After the score, they cleared the place out.

"Looks that way." Hamish's voice sounded muffled. "Could you refresh the screen, Izzy? I can't see anyone."

But Izzy didn't move. She had hugged the tablet to her chest. She was looking at Darius, her eyes wide with fear. "It's okay," she said. "It's okay."

"It is definitely *not* within a million miles of *okay*," March spit out.

Darius looked up from his phone. "His website is down. Text bounced back."

"He's long gone," March said. He looked out the window. "Probably on our yacht."

"You called it, March. I have information that he's operating in the Cayman Islands," Hamish said. "You were in Europe for ten days casing the job. He worked fast. I don't know who bought the place. It has a certain black market smell to it. Probably sold it to someone for cash."

Darius backed up and sat down in a heap. He dropped his head in his hands.

Izzy put the tablet on the counter and went to sit next to Darius. She leaned against him, but for once, he didn't acknowledge her.

"He said to put it all in a trust," Darius said hoarsely, his head between his knees. "He said that's what rich people do. They find tax-free investments, shelters, a portfolio with a thirty percent return."

"So we're flat broke?" Jules asked. "Just what we have in our pockets?"

"A thief is never broke," Hamish said. "Just temporarily out of funds. But, yeah."

March felt as though the top of his head would come off. The money, the accounts, the home Alfie had bought, the life he had dreamed? Just gone? Just like that?

Everything they'd built, everything they'd imagined. Gone.

A volcano of rage roared through March, and he spun to face Darius. "How could you let this happen? How could you be so *stupid*?"

Darius flinched, as if he'd hit him. A look came over his face, one that March had never seen before. Vulnerable. Young. Lost.

"Hey!" Izzy said, rising to her feet. "We don't talk to each other like *parents*! That's a rule!"

"Do you know what you gave away?" March yelled, ignoring Izzy. "Everything! Not just our home, but our *safety*! Do you know what money buys? Security, and passports, and IDs, and the *future*!"

"I know that!" Darius shouted, his face contorted. "Don't you think I know that?"

"It was almost *twenty million dollars*!"

"I know how much it was! What am I supposed to do?"

"Get it back!" March stamped his foot hard. He lowered his voice and took a step toward Darius. He pounded the wall. "I want it back. I want it all! I want the couches and the computers and the furniture and the blankets and the pillows and the dartboard." With every item, he hit the wall with his fist. "I want the games and the trapeze and the sixteen-foot-long dining table. I want the waffle iron and the sneakers and the snacks. I want Jules's wooden hairbrush and Izzy's stuffed chipmunk."

"We never even used the waffle iron," Izzy said.

"You fell for the most basic con there is," March said bitterly. "There's nothing between us and the street now. It means we're just another bunch of homeless grifter kids. We're nobody now. We're *nothing*. And it's all because of *you*!"

Izzy put her hands over her ears. "Stop it!" Tears ran down her face, and she sobbed. "Please, stop it, March."

Jules came to his side. She put her hand on his wrist. He shook her off. Why should he stop? Just because Darius looked crushed, because Izzy looked scared, because Jules was warning him he'd gone too far? He didn't care.

"It's too late to stop it," March said. "We're done."

21

WHAT NOW?

If it hadn't been for Hamish, March didn't know how they would have dealt with the next step. It was Hamish who offered them his condo, said he'd buy them tickets to Florida.

It was Hamish who reminded them that they still had the sapphire.

They had something left, at least.

Rage churned in March's stomach. He was furious at himself for letting it happen. For not asking the right questions. For not taking some of the money and putting it away someplace safe.

Never forget your walking-away money.

The group fractured into twos. He stuck with Jules, and Izzy, as always, stayed close to Darius. They left the house they'd once owned and trudged to the subway. They headed back to the airport.

On the rattling train March's anger drained, and a sinkhole of fear opened up inside him. It was a feeling he'd known all through his childhood. When chips were down and money was gone. *What next?*

Home was the place they'd created together. There, they'd felt safe. Now he felt small, just a chump in a hard city that ground and gnashed around him like a machine.

He remembered Dukey's words: *You're kids.*

Gone. The river would glint outside the windows without him. His key wouldn't open the front door.

For a year, March had woken up thinking, *Okay, Pop,*

I'm sad, but at least I followed through. I found Jules. We found your diamond. We made a home. Bummer you're not here, though.

Now he was back on the run. It was almost like losing Alfie all over again.

The Miami airport felt like a dream in a tropical land. People ambled along the corridors in shorts and sandals and baggy T-shirts. They passed a tiled wall full of blue and silver fake fish chasing one another in endless, lifeless loops. The lowering sun was too bright outside the windows, glinting off metal and glass.

Nobody spoke as they exited to the humid Miami air. March scanned the arriving cars for Hamish's frizzy silver ponytail.

"We'll have to wait," Darius said.

"Your powers of observation are amazing," March said.

Darius and Izzy drifted closer to the curb.

Jules gave him an exasperated look. "That was lousy."

March pressed his lips together. "What am I supposed to do?"

"Just . . . give him the *tiniest* of breaks. He's suffering!"

"You think *he's* suffering?"

"Look, we all are, okay? It was a lot to lose."

"Which is kinda *my point?*"

"Don't you dare tell me to move!" The voice floated above the sounds of car horns and the squeals of hellos. It even cut through Jules's air of exasperation.

"I'm picking up my boy, so I am *not* moving until I see his face!"

Darius whirled around, panic on his face.

Jules gestured. "It's Mikki!"

A short, muscular woman in a tank top proclaiming MIAMI HEAT stood arguing with an airport employee, a crumpled sign in her hand. "You have some *compassion*," she said, stamping her foot.

"Mama, what are you doing here?" Darius asked.

"Baby!" Mikki Fray wrapped her arms around Darius. She came up to his collarbone, but she rocked him like a toddler. "I'm so glad to see you."

"I'm glad to see you, too, but —"

"What, I'm not going to pick you up at the airport?"

"But I didn't tell you I was —"

"I got my ways, Darius P. Fray. What kind of mother do you think I am?"

"Do you really want me to answer that question?"

"No, I do not," Mikki said, smacking him on the arm, then hugging him again.

Mikki Fray had been in prison three times. Although she was one of the best wheelmen in the business, she wasn't so great at picking friends. She'd lost custody of Darius, and he'd been raised by his grandmother until bouncing into foster care. Mikki had pulled off a mysterious job a year ago and had made enough to retire — she claimed. Since then March had watched Darius waiting for her to ask him to join her in Florida, to finally give him a home, but the call never came. She was totally cool with his living on his own. She loved him fiercely, but she was happy for him to stay out of her way.

The airport worker waved his walkie-talkie. "Move along, ma'am. There's a time limit on how long you can stop here."

"I am moving along. Can't you see me move? Honey,

people should *pay* to watch my moves. Now leave me alone while I hug this sweet girl." Mikki grabbed Izzy and hugged her.

She released Izzy and hugged Jules and March. "C'mon, everybody, I've got a car right here. Unfortunately my T-bird had a little altercation with another vehicle this very afternoon. But lucky for me, I got a ride! Come and meet my driver."

"But, Mama, we're supposed to get picked up —"

"I know all about that. Your friend called me, asked if I could pick you up. I said, 'Are you kidding? They're all coming to Miami and Darius didn't tell me?'"

"Spur of the moment," March said.

Mikki waggled a forefinger at him. "I'll get it out of you, don't you fret."

She led them to a dented pickup truck that had probably once been blue, or maybe brown. It was hard to tell. "This is Dimmy," she said, sweeping an arm to indicate a stocky man leaning against the car, dressed in baggy shorts that reached his knees. He wore a backward baseball cap. "I smashed into his car!"

"Actually I smash into *her* car," Dimmy said in a thick Eastern European accent. "She's so nice, she won't say this."

"He's Ukrainian — or maybe Siberian, I forget — but what he is really, he's a Good Samaritan," Mikki said. "He drove me here for free!"

Dimmy's goofy smile was directed at Mikki. He shot her a look of intense admiration from his puppy-dog brown eyes. "I recognize wonderful woman in three seconds exactly. Mother devotion, so anxious to get her child. Mikki, which one is your son?"

Darius looked at March, then Jules, then Izzy. "Guess."

"Ha! Stupid question. Right? Only boy of color. But I'll tell you — the handsomest! Son of Mikki is best-looking! Oops, you are very good-looking, too," he said to March. He reached for Izzy's backpack. "Come on, plenty of room."

"Where did you find this guy, Mama?" Darius asked in a low tone.

Mikki beamed. "On I-95! It was my lucky day!"

"No, mine," Dimmy said, overhearing her. "Because I met such a beautiful lady."

"Stop it!"

"No, you stop it. Accept your beauty!" Dimmy waved his arms. "Not enough beauty to go around in world. Even in Florida, tropical paradise that hangs like pretty girl's braid from rest of country. Come on, Mikki's kids. Squeeze in."

Mikki ushered them toward the truck, steering them out of Dimmy's earshot. "I'm an accountant, you got that? An *accountant*. Not a wheelman. And you're kids on a vacation. No matter what you're doing, I don't want to know. You're ordinary normal kids while you're here. Got that?"

They all nodded.

"We're always normal ordinary kids," Izzy said. "In our own minds, anyway."

22

MIAMI HEAT

Mikki would not hear of them crashing at Hamish's condo. If they were in Florida, they had to stay with her, or else.

"Dimmy will drive you to your friend's place tomorrow, but you got to eat dinner with me tonight. I haven't seen you in forever, and that's just terrible."

"Well, you could have visited, Mama," Darius said.

"I know, but I'm so busy." Mikki patted his knee. "You know how it is around tax time for accountants."

Dimmy dropped them at a one-story concrete house with a red tile roof and a tiny pool in back, then waved cheerfully as he drove off, yelling, "Enjoy palm tree paradise, you dudes!"

"Isn't he sweet?" Mikki sighed.

"Adorable," Darius said.

Mikki pushed open the door to the house. It was half-furnished, even though she'd lived there a year. The yard was overgrown. If she'd made money from her last job, it couldn't have been much. She still played the lottery every week. She swore to Darius that she was out of "the criminal enterprise business," but she'd said that before.

"Look at my car!" she exclaimed, flourishing her phone. "It's proof! It's a turquoise vintage T-bird! What kind of a fool crook would pick a flashy car like that? Now, let's talk about you. How's New York?" She narrowed her eyes at Darius. "Something's wrong with you. I can see it. You got boyfriend trouble?"

"Nothing like that. I'm just hanging out, Mama."

"Okay. What do you think about inviting Dimmy over for dinner tomorrow?" Mikki peered at Darius nervously. "What, you don't like him?"

"I don't know him. And neither do you. Didn't you just meet him?"

"Well, yes, but we had a soul connection."

Darius snorted.

"Listen, Mr. I'm-Too-Cool-for-School, when you go straight, you know what happens? Nobody to talk to. You can't hang, all right? Too much temptation. I told my friend Shonda, don't call me for a while, girl, because I don't even want to *hear* the news."

"He seems like he's a few shots short of a venti latte."

"What? You know I don't drink fancy coffee."

"He's a bowl of chowder without the clams."

"It's the language barrier!"

Darius raised an eyebrow. Mikki shrugged. "Okay. He fits his name. But I'm not looking for Einstein. I'm looking for some company, that's all." She looked to March, Jules, and Izzy for support. "We're all just looking for some company, am I right?"

Darius sighed. "All right, Mama, whatever makes you happy. At least he's not in the family business."

"That's what I'm saying! He's a hard worker, just like me! Except legal! Well, except for the whole green card thing. He works two jobs, livery cab and landscaper! He's going for the American dream: work hard, get nowhere, win the lottery! Look, I got a house, a car, some money in the bank — you need money, baby? I'll write you a check right now. What are you all doing here anyway?"

They all spoke at the same time.

"Vacation," Jules said.

"Visiting relatives," Izzy said.

"Surfing," March said.

"Seeing you, of course," Darius said.

Mikki tapped a purple fingernail on the Formica. "Uh-huh. I'll tell you something. You four look like you came here for a funeral. You're on the straight and narrow, then?"

"Straight as Robin Hood's arrow, Mama."

"Don't you go saying that, I say that. And you know Robin Hood was a crook. This boy knows how to play me!" Laughing, Mikki leaned over and swatted him on the side of the head, then landed a smacking kiss in the same spot. "I'm going to the fish store for some grouper. Just stay out of trouble until I get back!"

23

TROUBLE

The next morning, Hamish's face was flushed as he carefully put the sapphire back on the black velvet cloth. It flashed blue fire with an ice-cold star at its heart.

"It's the Morning Star," he said in a hushed voice. "No doubt about it. We are sitting in the presence of one of the three most famous sapphires in the world."

March let out the breath he'd been holding. At the last minute, he'd started to worry that the gem was fake.

They sat in the living room of Hamish's small condo. It was like being in a rain forest. Almost everything was green — carpet, sofa, kitchen chairs. Huge paintings of tropical birds hung on the walls and leaned against the shelving unit. Hamish had explained that his wife, Keiko, had taken up painting. A sweating glass of iced tea sat next to a stack of celebrity magazines.

"What an amazing piece of luck," Hamish said.

March cocked his head as Hamish's remark hit him. He glanced at Jules. She raised an eyebrow. He heard Alfie's voice in his head.

Sure, you can trust Hamish. But never forget he's always out for the deal.

Jules hitched herself up on Hamish's round white dining table and swung her legs. "This is some lucky luck, Hamster," she observed. "You hear about some rich guy selling a whole bunch of diamonds, and — whoa — the most famous sapphire in the world happens to be there, too, and you didn't even know it." She whistled. "Unbelievable."

"And when I show it, you identify it immediately," March pointed out. "Over a computer connection. Incredible."

"Anybody for green tea?" Hamish asked. "I have those granola cookies you like. Keiko isn't here, but she gave me the recipe —"

"You *planned* this," March said. "You knew the French guy had the sapphire! You tricked us!"

"I merely withheld one piece of information —"

"The most important piece!"

"— in order to allay any fears you might have, before you had them —"

"That's ridiculous!"

"— and make our fortune!"

"We already have a fortune!" March caught himself. He threw a look at Darius. "Well. We *did*."

Hamish waved his hands in the air. "I must clear the negative energy. If we focus on negativity, we can't go forward in life with positiveness."

"Did you know the Top Cats were after the jewels?" March asked.

"No!" Hamish put a hand on his heart.

"Well, the feds now think we're with the Top Cat gang," March said. He quickly explained about Agent Dukey.

"That is unfortunate news," Hamish mused. "But the Top Cats are a European gang. No doubt after the diamonds. I think we're safe to proceed."

"Proceed with what?" Jules asked. "We said no to stealing the other rocks, remember?"

"But surely, the circs have changed due to your unfortunate situation."

"That's one way to put it," March said. "Though *complete freaking disaster* might be good, too."

"March," Hamish said, "we have a saying in the criminal world. Might make you feel better: 'You always lose your first fortune.'"

"That's really comforting."

"It should be. Because you will get another one. Especially," Hamish said, leaning back and resting his hands on his belly, "if you listen to wise old me."

"Family is more important than money," Izzy said, with a quick glance at March.

"Tell us about the job, Ham," Darius broke in.

"Well. I did some research after you showed me the stone, and I think I've located the second one! And, oddly enough, it's right here in Miami!"

"That *is* odd," Jules said. She tossed a copy of *Miami Social Sheet* on the table next to Hamish. "Take a look at page fourteen."

Hamish grinned nervously. "I never read that rag. I buy it for Keiko. You know I don't read about celebrities. I have to keep my aura clean. We only have so much brain space. Gossip, pro football, reality TV, Miley Cyrus — I just have to block *some* things out so I can concentrate on the good things in life. Like sun salutations and smoothies."

Jules jumped off the table and flipped to the page. "Trini Abbo, the former model who married the most mysterious man in Miami, Terrence Abbo . . ."

"Minor celebs, indeed —"

"Look at her *neck*."

"Hmm. Lovely piece of jewelry. Do you think it's an engagement present?"

"I think it's a star sapphire." Jules tossed the magazine down in disgust. "And this magazine is from a *month* ago. You've been planning this job. When were you going to tell us? You didn't bring us here to help us out. You brought us here to steal that necklace!"

"Oh, Hamish." Izzy shook her head. "Not very up-front of you."

"Ultimately the hilltop of truth is my guiding principle, but sometimes you need a . . . uh, little switchback to get there," Hamish said. "And it's for your own good! You might not have tried for the Morning Star if you'd known! Now we have it, and that's good, right?"

"Ham, my man," Darius said, shaking his head, "I don't think you're getting the point. We just want you to be straight with us."

"What about —" Izzy started.

"If the feds are watching us, how can we risk it?" Jules asked.

"If you could just tell us about —" Izzy said again.

"If you knew about the Miami sapphire a month ago, you've been planning this for a while," March said. "Do you have a buyer for all three?"

"I'll get to that," Hamish said. "First . . . well, there's something I haven't mentioned."

Izzy leaned in. "Tell us about the curse."

24

ZILLAH

Hamish's smile tilted. "What curse?"

Izzy crossed her arms. She was barely five feet tall, but when she wanted to, she had the propulsive heft of a linebacker.

"Oh, *that* curse," Hamish said with a nervous chuckle. "What's a famous jewel without a curse? This one is a great story! Back in the Dark Ages, the three sapphires were stolen by a sailor. He pried them from a sacred statue of a goddess in Ceylon. So, he does what sailors do — he gives them to a girl back home. Her name was Zillah, and she used them as healing stones. Except the villagers were spooked by the cures, so they called her a witch."

"That's terrible," Izzy said.

"Healers were often accused of being witches," Jules interjected. "Strong women are often feared by stupid men. Happened all the time back then. Still happening." She shrugged. "Progress."

Hamish held up a finger. "So they stole the gems and tied her to a big rock and threw her in the river. If she floated, she was a witch and they'd burn her. If she drowned, she was, uh, dead. So, she drowned. Let me tell you, those were harsh dudes back in the olden days. Before she died, Zillah was understandably ticked off. She laid a curse on whoever owned the stones. Ready?"

Ham stood, ready to recite.

"*I curse your bones, I curse these stones.*

By rules of three I decree
Them that own cannot atone.
Fortune and hearthstone, then fealty fly
'Til hearts are riven and death is nigh.
Break these stones and ye shall know
How even the mighty be brought so low.
See my mark upon thy floor
And I shall haunt forevermore."

"What does it all mean?" Darius asked.

"The rule of three is the stones," Hamish said. "Separately, the stones bring bad juju. All together? Death. *But* the stones *need* to be together — there's a powerful force binding them."

"Fortune, hearthstone, fealty," Izzy repeated. "Money, home, loyalty, right? We've already lost two of those." Her hands flew to her mouth. "Since we stole the sapphire! That's why it happened!"

"The sapphire didn't lose our fortune," March said. "I think we all know who did that."

Darius glowered at March.

"But it all happened right after we stole it!" Izzy said. "Who knows when they stole our stuff . . . it could have been that very morning! And you said you almost got your head cut off, March. Just like Anne Boleyn!"

"Why would anyone *want* these jewels, if everyone ends up broke, friendless, and dead?" Jules asked.

"And what does 'my mark upon thy floor' mean?" Darius asked.

"Oh, nothing." Hamish brushed the air with his fingers. "It's said that Zillah haunts you if you have the stones. She drowned, right? There are stories of finding wet footprints in a house in the middle of the night. Stuff like that."

"Or a blowing curtain where there's no wind," Izzy said.

"Let's not let our imaginations get away from us," Hamish said. "I believe in curses, but not in ghosts."

"I feel her," Izzy whispered. "She's with us right now."

They all grew quiet.

"This is ridic —" Hamish started. Just then a painting of an orange macaw flew off the wall and crashed onto the floor.

25

NO SUCH THING AS GHOSTS

"What. Was. That," Darius said.

"Ah. Um. Heh." Hamish chortled nervously. "I'm so bad at hanging things." He quickly threw a dish towel over the sapphire.

Izzy tucked herself up into a ball, her hands clasped around her shins. "It reminds me of my grandmother in San Juan," she said. "Once she saw the ghost of Doña Ana walking the hall in the El Convento Hotel. Doña Ana passed right through her. My grandmother was young then, with long black hair. It turned completely white that night."

"I don't believe in ghosts," Hamish repeated. "Uh, most of the time."

"Jules has a point," Darius said. "Who would want the sapphires? Plenty of pretty stones in the world without tangling with curses and ghosts."

"You know how it is with curses," Hamish said. "The rule of three, the rule of seven. The rule of seven counteracts the rule of three."

"Oh, sure," Darius said. "Everybody knows that."

"If you employ the rule of seven, you get fantastic *good* luck. Which brings me to the last owner of the necklace. Sir Roland Chervil Ransome, born Reg Mifflewhite in the East End of London."

"Doesn't he own that airline?" Darius asked.

"And a car company, and a technology company, and he's building a rocket to go to the moon," Hamish said. "He built his company from nothing. About twenty years ago, he bought the Gate of Heaven necklace for his wife after his first major deal. And he had *crushingly* bad luck. Plus, his wife made him sell their house —"

"Because it was haunted, I bet," Izzy said.

"Well, she thought so. Anyway, he went broke. Terrible debt. Wife left him. Best friend betrayed him. Financial manager fleeced him."

"Well, *that* part sounds familiar," March said.

"Thanks for reminding us, Marcello," Darius said sourly. "'Cause we almost forgot for a full second."

"Luck swings both ways, like a gate," Hamish said, waving his hand back and forth. "But this was a series of calamities that went beyond the beyond. It was then that he took the necklace seriously. Instead of selling it, he went to a psychic. She told him if he broke down the necklace but kept the stones together in seven nesting boxes carved from the nutmeg tree from the original shrine, the goddess would be appeased, and thus Zillah's power would be cast away." Hamish shrugged. "So he did it. Went all the way to Sri Lanka, found the nutmeg tree near the original shrine, had the boxes made."

"And?" March asked. He was interested in spite of himself.

"The power of the stones switched! His luck reversed! He got his money back!"

"And his wife?" Izzy asked.

"Nah! He got a younger, prettier one!"

Jules did a backflip onto the couch in the way she had of making it look easy. She landed with her head on the pillow and her feet up. "Personally, I hoped we were done with curses forever."

March felt a shiver race down his spine. They'd tangled with a curse a little over a year ago — one that said he and Jules were destined to die before their thirteenth birthday. They didn't believe it. Not at first. Not until the moonstones started to weigh them down, glow in rooms without a moon, darken their dreams into nightmares.

So yeah, he had seen curses in action. He couldn't say he didn't believe.

"Unfortunately, curses go with gems the way peanut butter goes with jelly," Hamish said.

"Doesn't it scare you?" Izzy asked.

"Dear Izzy, I have a great respect for curses, but I also have a great respect for large amounts of cash. This deal seems worth the risk."

"So this dude is desperate to get them back?" Darius asked.

"Exactly! Are you ready for what he'll pay?"

"I don't care," Jules said.

"How much?" March asked.

"Fifty million dollars." Hamish rolled out the words and then licked his lips as though he'd just finished a triple-scoop ice-cream cone. With sprinkles.

"How come so much?" Jules asked.

"Because priceless is expensive!" Hamish cried. "And because he *believes*. As soon as those sapphires were stolen, his luck changed again." Hamish made the swinging-gate gesture again. "He blames the gems. He *needs* the gems. He wants the good luck back. *He wants these sapphires.*" Hamish rubbed his hands together. "Desperate and rich. The perfect client."

March had that itchy feeling that meant this job was trouble. Unfortunately that didn't stop him from being tempted. What choice did they have? They were busted. And three perfect sapphires were within reach. He felt the call of the last big score, the one that would thrill him and test him and save him. No better feeling in the world, Alfie used to say.

"Fifty million isn't worth anything if you're in prison," Jules pointed out.

Izzy nodded. But Darius had an interested look on his face. A look, March guessed, exactly like his own.

Darius slid the magazine over and studied the picture of Terrence and Trini Abbo. "Tell us about the mark," he said.

26

MAJOR BAD

"Major bad dude," Hamish said. "Karma will set him back a thousand years and turn him into a newt. Started out as a mercenary and turned himself into a 'military advisor' to the worst dictators on the planet. Basically he was a one-man reign of terror. He has about a billion-gazillion dollars, so he retired. Found himself a wife in Miami — half his age, a former model named Trini. The star sapphire necklace was an engagement present. She doesn't know it, but he bought the stone — the diamonds, too — on the black market and had it designed just for her. The diamonds make up stars and the Evening Star is supposed to be the moon. It's vulgar, if you ask me, but nobody's asking. Anyway, the billion bucks means he made himself a nice little compound in Miami with top-level security. Infrared scopes, sniper on the roof, motion detectors. And bodyguards."

March pushed the magazine away. "Are you *kidding* me? You want us to boost a stone off some billionaire, murdering dictator?"

"Advisor."

"Can we go back to the snipers for a sec?" Jules asked.

"On paper, it's not good," Hamish agreed. "The guy is seriously paranoid. Which is probably wise, seeing how many people want to kill him. So forget trying to get his schedule. He has a fleet of cars with blacked-out windows. Decoy cars. Mixes up his routine constantly."

"Is there *any* good news?" March asked.

"Of course there is!" Hamish exclaimed. "Would I place my favorite kids in danger? It's a cakewalk! And here's why: golf."

"Golf," Jules repeated.

"The guy lives for golf. He's a member of the most exclusive club in Miami. Million-dollar membership fee. And she goes where he goes. Think about it — it's out in the open, and I'm betting there's more than one exit. He's relaxed, she's relaxed, they're not expecting anything. Bodyguards get bored and hot. Look." Hamish fished out a magazine from a pile by the table. He flipped open a copy of *Miami Lifestyle* and pushed it toward them.

They all leaned forward to study the picture. The woman was striking, with long dark wavy hair. She was wearing a tiny pink polo shirt, a white miniskirt, and golf shoes. The sapphire rested against her throat, the diamond chain winking in the sunlight. Terrence had his hand on her arm as though he was stopping her from talking or moving. In his hand, the golf club looked like a weapon. Trini's smile looked strained. March noted all of this, even though it was just a picture of two handsome people standing under a palm tree. He glanced at Jules. She'd seen the same thing. Her gray eyes darkened.

"He's a creep," she said.

"Indubitably," Hamish agreed. "He looted countries out of their treasuries, and she hitched herself to his money and his protection." He shrugged. "It's an old story."

"How did you find out about this sapphire in the first place?" Darius asked.

"Yoga!" Hamish smiled at each of them in turn. "Gives flexibility plus occasional professional tips! I'm in a regular class when I'm here in Miami. I got to talking to a guy there,

Milton Silver. Eighty-five years old, and you should see his downward dog. And his soul! Such a pure aura. Pink and gold. Where was I? Ah! He tells me about this yoga teacher — so exclusive you can't get into the classes. You've got to be young and connected to get in, he says, and he really works up a head of steam about this, because, you know, it's counter to the whole *spirit* of yogic practice, okay? They call it 'model yoga,' because everybody is young and thin. So I look up the class, because I'm thinking, hey, maybe I could do Milt a favor and get him in. And there's a photo." He held out his phone. "And I see this."

Trini Abbo stood next to an incredibly fit and gorgeous woman in her fifties. They were both dressed in yoga gear. The caption read, *Yogi to the stars Mirabelle Ralston greets student Trini Abbo, a model and actress in Miami.*

The star sapphire gleamed against Trini's tan throat.

"I almost fell over, let me tell you. I couldn't believe it was really what I was seeing, so I've been staking out the yoga studio. After class she goes to this coffee place with her gal pal and they chat for maybe twenty minutes while her bodyguards drink coffee and look glum at a table in the corner. There! I gave you so much info, this will be a piece of cake! I would go again, but I'm staying away from caffeine!"

"That's all you've got?" March said.

Hamish spread his hand. "For your criminal genius mind, it should be plenty!"

"Uh-huh. And what about the *third* sapphire? Do you know where it is?"

"Ha!" Hamish beamed at March. "I've been waiting for you to ask me that question. You're a Cancer. *So* intuitive. What's your rising sign?"

"Impatience."

"I know where the third is. Easy job. Easy peasy, mango squeezy. I'll fill you in when we decide to go ahead."

"*If.*"

"I think the golf club is our best bet," Darius said. "There's got to be some info on when tee times are, or whatever they call it. We could do a smash-and-grab on the twenty-fifth hole, or something."

"That would work, if it wasn't for the fact that there are only eighteen holes," March said.

"Do I look like I grew up playing golf, Marcello?" Darius asked.

"I would not describe this as a slam dunk, Ham," Jules said. "There's about a hundred things that could go wrong."

"That's March's department," Hamish said. "He sees the hundred things. He plans for the hundred things. And then it all works."

March rubbed his forehead. He felt the pressure of the decision building in his head. He didn't like these odds. It was what Alfie would call a "walk away" situation. Still, the knowledge of what they'd lost was pounding inside him. Without money, where would they go? How far would the proceeds of one broken-up sapphire take them?

He knew the answer: not far enough.

"I've got a bad feeling about this," he said. "Too much security, too much I can't predict. Plus snipers." He was about to add *but we need to think about it* when Jules jumped in, a relieved look on her face.

"I'm with March," Jules said. "I vote no."

Darius shrugged. "We can't do it without you two," he said. "So . . ."

Ham crashed back against his chair. "Well. That's that."

"Hey!" Izzy sprang to her feet. "What about me? Don't I get a voice?"

"Of course you do, Iz," March said. "It's just that you never . . . usually . . . vote."

Izzy lifted her chin. "Well, I'm voting. I say let's do it."

27

DO IT FOR BIG D

Everyone turned and looked at Izzy. She had never spoken up like that before.

"But first, I'm hungry," Izzy said. "Ham, can you get some Cuban sandwiches? I've always wanted to try Cuban sandwiches. Even though I'm Puerto Rican. I don't know what time it is in France, but it feels like dinner."

"Excellent idea!" Hamish grabbed his keys. "Darius, give me a hand?"

Darius looked at Izzy, confusion on his face. "Uh, sure. We'll be right back. Don't discuss anything while we're gone."

As soon as the door closed behind them, tiny Izzy strode toward March, her hands on her hips.

"Why are you hesitating? We *have* to do this job," Izzy said.

Jules unwound herself from her position on the couch. "You're right, Iz," she agreed.

"I know," March said. "Because we're broke."

They exchanged that look that girls do when they silently agree that boys are stupid.

"I'm not doing it because of that," Jules said. "I'm doing it for Darius."

Izzy nodded. "He needs to do this. He needs to get the money back."

"The money's *gone*, thanks to him," March said furiously.

"We get that," Jules said. "So does he. Especially since you keep mentioning it!"

"I don't think I can mention it *enough*," March said.

"Look, I'm upset, too. We all are, but I'm not *punishing* him." She held up a finger. "And *don't* tell me he deserves it. Nobody deserves what you're dishing out. He didn't mean to do it!"

"What's the difference?" March asked. He slumped on the couch. "It's still gone."

"There is a difference," Izzy insisted. "He was trying to do a good thing, not a bad thing. That's when you need to forgive people! You called him stupid," she added softly.

March winced. He wished he could take that word back. He wished he could take back the memory of Darius's face when he'd said it.

"His father called him stupid all the time," Izzy said. "I know you didn't mean it. But now he feels like he's useless. We have to make him feel better. And the only way is if we get our money back. I'm scared we could lose him. I *mean* it."

The girls stood in front of March, a jury of two. "Okay, I get what you're saying, but I'm supposed to be not mad anymore? *He lost my father's legacy!*"

His hands balled into fists, and he squeezed as hard as he could, trying to stop the tears that suddenly pricked his eyes. His face was hot. When he thought of Alfie picking out that apartment, dreaming of a life he could give his kids, he wanted to howl.

"*Our* father," Jules said quietly.

Izzy sat next to him and, to March's surprise, put her arms around him. She hugged him hard, and he felt the tears he'd been holding back fill his eyes.

"I know," she said. "So does Darius."

"Why can't he say he's sorry, then?"

"Because sometimes sorry is too big to say."

28

KETCHUP AND PICKLES

The next day, the gang sat around the pool, drying off in the sunshine. They had slept long and hard, and the fog of jet lag plus shock was lifting. March and Darius were speaking again, but it felt like a struggle. Would they ever be able to get back to their easy friendship? March remembered fun afternoons that seemed to last forever. He'd taught D how to pick a lock and alter a passport without detection. Darius had taught him how to make a fart noise with his hands, a necessary part of his education that Alfie had missed.

Jules disappeared into the house and reappeared with a dish of pickles, a bowl of potato chips, and a saucer of ketchup.

The noise of a weed-whacker came to them faintly. Dimmy had shown up with it, saying he'd noticed Mikki's lawn needed help. His face fell when they told him that Mikki was out, but he brightened when Izzy added that this way, the lawn cleanup would be a surprise.

He flung out his arms. "Americans, they love surprises! In America, surprises are always happy!" His face deflated. "In my country, they are always bad." He put on his noise-canceling headphones and sighed.

"Have a chip, Dimmy," Jules said, patting him on the back.

"WHAT?" he yelled.

Now Jules put a slice of pickle on a chip and finished with a dollop of ketchup. She caught March's look. "Don't judge. So, now that we're in, what's the plan?"

"Know your mark," Izzy said. "Alfie's rule number one."

"Exactly," March said. "Know his routine, know what he likes for breakfast, know when he gets his mail. Know when he takes a walk, know when he picks his nose."

"Gross," Jules said.

"You're eating chip-pickle sandwiches, and you call that gross?" March snatched a chip and crunched. "Look, basically, thieves trip up in a million ways, but the main way they screw up is planning. Most people have routines. They go to work at the same time. They go to the gym, they go for a jog . . . usually at the same times."

"Except for guys who are wanted in five countries," Jules said.

"Exactly. He knows if people are after him, he has to mix it up. Not do the same thing every day at the same time. Send out decoy cars. He's used to living that way."

"That café where Trini sometimes goes after yoga? I mapped it online. Not good. On a dead end," Izzy said. "Only one way out. And a police station on the next block."

Deep in thought, March took a chip and added a pickle with ketchup. *Crunch.* It wasn't bad.

"You see? You gotta trust me," Jules said.

"I trust you. I just don't trust pickles. They belong on the *side.* They're a sneaky veg."

"They aren't a vegetable, they're a condiment."

"Right. And I'm not a thief, I just borrow things without permission."

Izzy pushed her tablet across the table with a satellite map of the golf club. "Here's the prob — the club is super private. One entrance with a guard and a gate. Employee entrance on the side with what looks to be a key-card entry. Surrounded on three sides with an electric fence concealed by a twenty-foot-high privacy hedge. One side fronts a river. Plus it's so exclusive their website doesn't say anything. I can't get a staff list or any email addresses. And I could only find a few photographs on the web."

"We can't go into that place blind," March said. "We'll get picked off in two minutes."

"So what do we do?" Jules brightened. "Pull a Blanchard and parachute in?"

The rest of them rolled their eyes. Ever since March had told them the story of Gerald Blanchard, who had parachuted onto the roof of a palace in Austria and made off with the diamond and pearl Sisi Star, the most famous jewel in Austrian history, Jules had hoped for parachuting glory.

"Outside my skill set," March said. "Sorry."

Darius tapped the tablet. "We could do an Orange Vest with a twist."

"I know about Orange Vest," Jules said. "That's the guy who put the ad on Craigslist for construction workers. Said to show up in an orange vest. A bunch of people showed up. So after he pulled off the heist, he just put on a vest and got away in the crowd."

"Right," March said. "But what would a whole bunch of people show up for in Miami? To a golf course? Maybe if we throw in a Joe Loutsenheizer . . ."

"What's a Loutsenheizer?" Izzy asked.

"That's what Alfie called acting like a loudmouth for a diversion," March said. He tapped the table, thinking hard. "Lots of problems with this one."

Izzy straightened. "Hey, it's like what that guy said . . . who was the guy, the politician in World War Two, the British guy?"

"Patton," Darius said.

"The Red Baron," Jules said.

March dropped his head in his hands. "We really need some homeschooling."

"Churchill!" Izzy said triumphantly. "'Never, never, never give up.' That's what he said. That's three *nevers*, so you know he meant it."

Darius put his finger on a twisting blue line. "Remember how Orange Vest got away?"

"Right," March said. "Not a bad idea."

"Amazing that I thought of it," Darius mumbled.

The buzz of Dimmy's weed-whacker was gone. Maybe it had been for a while. He was planting something not far away and gave a cheerful wave. The quiet of the afternoon descended on March, soft and easy, and he heard birdsong. He swatted at a lazy fly circling his head. The fly dive-bombed into the ketchup.

Break it down.

First. Get them where you want them to be.

Second. Diversion.

Third. Lift the stone.

Fourth. Getaway.

March grabbed the bowl of chips and placed it in the center of the table. He laid out two pickle spears in a line on one side.

Jules, Izzy, and Darius looked at him hopefully.

He pointed to the bowl. "That's the club. Here's the river," he said, pointing to the pickle spears. "Orange Vest could work. The thief got away on an inflatable boat. But we have a bigger problem than the getaway. We'd have to have an exact time they're at the club, *ahead of time*. That's our only shot. And that's impossible."

"Maybe not," Izzy said.

29

THE HACK

Izzy spun around her tablet. She reached over and expanded a photo on a tabloid site. "Her wrist."

March and Jules leaned over. "Bracelet?"

Izzy shook her head. "One of those fitness trackers. I've been looking at all the photos I can find, and there are three things she never takes off — that necklace, her wedding ring, and the tracker."

"Well, we know she's serious about working out."

"I'm more interested in the information on that thing."

"Wait a second, Izzy." Jules grew suddenly intent. "Are you saying you can hack into a fitness band?"

"Well, I need some parameters," Izzy said. "It syncs with her mobile phone, right? So, if we identify the brand, and the info is set in cleartext, and she visits the same café regularly and uploads info on Wi-Fi — which we can kind of bet on, because it probably paired in the past — and if I'm there, I can run my software and load Wi-Fi traffic onto my computer, compress it, upload it, isolate the Mac address, strip out the Ethernet packets —"

"You can cut to the chase any time now, genius girl," Darius interrupted.

"— I can get inside and get all her info — when she wakes up, goes to sleep, works out, calories burned, maybe even what she eats and how much water she drinks —"

"You can get the time of her workouts at the golf club?" March asked.

Jules nodded. "Maybe there's a pattern; we just don't know it."

Izzy shrugged, her usual yes answer to a hacking job that seemed perfectly simple to her.

"Just get me within ten yards for about ten minutes," she said. "That's all I need."

30

GIVE ME WHAT'S REAL

The café was filled with what appeared to be a tribe of supermodels. The women spilled in, chatting and laughing, in their spandex and yoga gear. They held conversations while constantly flipping their hair, taking selfies, and checking their phones.

Trini Abbo sauntered in, chatting idly with her companion, who was also wearing yoga clothes and was equally gorgeous. Even from here March could see the star sapphire around Trini's neck. The diamonds flashed in the lights.

March took a bite of his doughnut. It tasted like a sponge. He was too nervous to appreciate food. Jules had already demolished one doughnut and was starting on her second.

Trini grabbed her coffee and made her way to a table in the corner, which her bodyguards had already staked out. They gathered up her yoga mat and sat at a nearby table. March knew that behind their dark glasses, their gazes were constantly roaming the place and checking the street outside. At the curb Trini's black SUV was pulled up in a loading zone, the engine running.

March glanced at Izzy at another table. She had her earbuds in and was tapping on the keys. A textbook called *Our Shared Heritage* was on the table, but he knew she was intently downloading as much information as she could get from people surfing the web on their phones. Somewhere in that information they would get the key to Trini's schedule. Izzy's head bobbed to the music supposedly in her ears.

Outside, Darius sipped on a juice, pretending to wait for a bus. He was there just to ensure that everything went smoothly. March always felt safer when Darius was nearby. He had an instinct for trouble, and he knew how to avoid it. Why had he failed so badly and trusted a crook?

"It's funny how I always depended on D to keep trouble away," March said. "Then he delivered it right to my door."

"That's a lot to depend on someone for," Jules said, munching on her doughnut. "Trouble makes up its own mind. You know what I was thinking? Hamish is right. It's *easy* to lose a fortune. I mean, when you're a thief. The only thing that can cut a diamond is another diamond. The only person who can scam a thief is another thief. Hard against hard, right? Darius got taken, but it could have happened to any of us."

"What? It wouldn't have happened to me."

"Not that way, maybe," Jules admitted. "But think about last year. We didn't know how to handle what we had. We were trying to hide, but we bought that whole building. That attracted too much attention, right off the bat. How long would we have gotten away with it? How many times did that nice guy in the bakery ask about our parents? What about the realtor who kept coming around? And the neighbor who asked all those questions when we put in the lap pool? We weren't as smart as you think."

"So it's okay that it's all gone?"

"No, it's *bad* that it's all gone. It's scary. But maybe next time we'll be more careful. We'll get it really right."

"We had it right," March said. "Alfie made it right."

Jules brushed crumbs off her lap. "Let me tell you something. I think it's great that Alfie had a dream to reunite us. I think it's terrific that he finally tried to put his kids first.

But he died before he could. How do we know it would have worked out?"

"What are you talking about?"

"How do you know he wouldn't have run out of money again? How do you know he wouldn't have invested in a crazy scheme to double his money? How do you know he wouldn't have lost everything? He did it, over and over, your whole life. Are you forgetting that?"

March felt as though Jules had driven a spike through his heart. He couldn't breathe for a minute. "I'm not forgetting anything!"

"Hey, be chill," Jules warned. "People are looking."

"You're wrong," he whispered fiercely. "Alfie would have hung on to that diamond, and the safe house. He was going to go straight."

Jules choked on a laugh. "Is that what you think?"

"That's what I *know*."

Jules blew out a breath. "What you remember and what's real . . . it's like two different things. Alfie left you in Paris for two weeks, you don't know whether he's alive or dead, and you're only ten? Come on. Not to mention he left me for ten *years*. Or that time in Hong Kong when he pulled off that big deal and then placed the whole amount on a roulette spin? What makes you think that would have changed?"

"It would have. I know it. He died for that moonstone. He did it for us. He would have gone straight because this time we would have all been together."

Jules let out a short bark of a laugh. "You don't know that! And it doesn't even make sense!"

"Just because things don't make sense doesn't mean they're not real."

"Now, *that* doesn't make sense."

March balled up his napkin. "When you give me what's real, I know it. That's the difference between you and me."

"What's *that* supposed to mean?"

"Nothing."

Just then Izzy stood and stretched. Then she shoved her computer in her tote bag and walked out.

"We've gotta go." March bundled up their trash and shoved it hard into the bin. He tried to catch his breath.

Jules was wrong. She was always hard on Alfie.

Izzy and Darius met up with them at the corner.

"She logs every workout, every calorie," she said. "She eats a papaya every day."

"The golf club?" Jules asked.

"She swims there twice a week. There *is* a pattern. One week it's Tuesday and Thursday; one week it's Wednesday and Friday. It's a Wednesday-Friday week."

March frowned. "That's the day after tomorrow."

Izzy nodded. "It's always at ten a.m."

"We've got a lot to do, then," March said. "Anything else?"

"After the swim — twenty minutes — she gets a smoothie. It's logged in every time after the swim, so she must go to the restaurant at the club." Izzy regarded him, her eyes narrowing. "Are you okay?"

"I'm okay."

"Do you have a plan?"

"Almost."

31

BAD DREAMS AND NIGHTMARES

That night March dreamed of the witch. She moved through the house like a shadow, casting shade and dread. Her gown was wet and dripping, and her long white feet left wet prints on the floor. She changed into a raven and landed on Jules's back, pecking her until she bled. The bird raised a bloody beak and a triumphant caw.

March woke, sweating, his heart pounding.

Just a dream, buddy. Go back to sleep now.

He burrowed under the blankets, missing his father's touch on his hair.

Izzy looked hollow-eyed the next morning as she splashed milk on her cereal. She caught a look at March's drawn face. "Nightmares?"

"Just a bad dream."

"What's the difference?"

"In a nightmare, you can't wake up."

"Oh." Izzy chewed thoughtfully. "I couldn't wake up. She took my breath. Zillah. She's around all the time now."

"Right." March upended the box over his bowl. "Ask her to get more Cheerios, will you?"

But even as he felt the satisfying crunch of *normal*, he couldn't get the image of Zillah out of his head.

SHOPPING LIST:
PLASTIC CONTAINER
JAM
FOUR SUN VISORS
WHITE SHORTS, WHITE POLOS, WHITE SNEAKERS
A COUPLE OF BOATS

They waited for Mikki to go to her Zumba class and then gathered at the kitchen table. March handed Jules a burner phone, one that they would toss immediately after using it.

"Time for a little social engineering," he said. It was what hackers called any method in which they used people skills to get passwords or emails or to bypass normal security routines. Sometimes rather than spend hours coding or trying to break firewalls, it was just easier to get someone to tell you what you needed to know.

Jules had mad gymnastic skills, but one thing they'd all discovered over the past year was how good she also was at impersonating an adult on the phone. If March was going to pretend to be a new employee, it would help to know the names of staff.

Jules closed her eyes and exhaled. Then she dialed the main number of the golf club and asked for the executive director. "And can you spell his last name, please?" she asked the receptionist. "I'm writing a label and don't want to get it wrong. P-E-T-E-R-S-O-N? Great. Can you connect me?"

A moment later, Jules changed her voice, making it deeper but a little spacey. "Hi, it's Brittany, over at Wholesale Distribution in Pompano? How are y'all doing today? Listen,

I've got the Tax ID number you requested right here. Do you have a pen? Oh. Gosh. I'm sorry, I *asked* for personnel. I guess they transferred wrong or something . . . I always talk to Terry. Is it Terry? I am *totally* spacing out her name — right, Marie. Don't you think Terry and Marie are similar names? Anyway, she asked for a Tax ID number, and I wanted to get it to her *mondo pronto*. Would you mind terribly giving me Marie's extension so I don't have to go through reception again? Two eleven? Great, got that. Oh, but now that I have you. Marie said that we needed to ask for the manager down at the spa to see if we need to add to the delivery? Nick! That was it! Nick C . . . C . . . oh, Nick Darwin, that's it, I have it written down right here. I'm sorry, you sound so busy, and here I am babbling. That's what my husband says to me all the time — he holds up his hand and says, *babble!* Thank you *so* much . . . was it Sue, you said? Ann Calloway, that's right. Thanks, Ann, you've been so super helpful, I'll let you go. Yes, you can transfer me to Marie, thanks, you're a doll!"

Jules hung up.

"Brilliant," March approved. "You got the CEO's assistant's name, the personnel director, and the spa manager."

"Candy security," Izzy said, repeating the term hackers used to describe a system that had a hard outer surface, but once you cracked it, the inside was smooth and deliciously easy.

"We just have to hope that Ann never checks with Marie in personnel and asks her about the ditzy idiot from Wholesale Distribution," Jules said.

"It looks like we're good to go," March said.

"How's your fly-catching system?" Darius asked.

"Worked like a charm. Can you ask Dimmy if he can give us a ride to the beach tomorrow morning?"

"Not Dimmy," Darius said. "I don't like that guy. I can drive, remember?" Darius had learned to drive over the last year, taking the train to New Jersey to learn from one of Hamish's many nephews, who happened to be the third-best wheelman in the tristate area, according to Hamish.

"It's better if the driver actually has a license," March said.

"Anyway, you don't like Dimmy because Mikki likes him," Izzy said.

"I don't like him because . . . because . . . he's pushy," Darius said. "He's always around."

"He's a hard worker," Jules said. "Mikki's yard looks really nice."

"I know you all think I'm just hating on him, but that's not it," Darius said. "I've seen this before. Mikki meets a guy, builds him up, and the next thing I know, she's an accessory."

"Anyway, why do we need Dimmy's truck?" Jules asked March.

"For the kayaks, of course," March said.

32

STAR SEARCH

March and Jules sat out by the pool. It was late. Stars appeared and disappeared through the shifting clouds of tropical sky. March tried to find the Big Dipper, but he'd never really learned the constellations. One of the many things Alfie didn't teach him.

Which is the North Star, Pop?

Do I look like a sailor, kid?

He remembered the sour twist to Alfie's mouth. He pushed away the memory. Was Jules right? Did he push away the times when Alfie had been impatient, or moody, or neglectful? Things didn't always go well. Money disappeared. People were double-crossers or let them down. There were plenty of apartments with not enough heat. Mice. Foldout couches for sleeping that smelled like sweat and mildew.

He didn't want to remember his life that way, didn't want to remember his father panicky or depressed. He wanted to remember him as his best friend, the fun guy who could turn a blue day around. He wanted to remember the five-star hotels and the first-class tickets and the shopping sprees.

"What did you mean when you said that I don't know what's real?" Jules asked.

"I was mad."

"Yeah. I got that memo. But you still meant it."

March let a few seconds go by. "I meant you don't know that Alfie loved you. I mean *know it*, like, in your bones."

There was a long pause. "And you do."

"Yeah," March said. "I do. And I know that he loved you, too."

Jules brushed at her face. It was either a tear or a mosquito. "I didn't know him. Not like you did."

"I didn't know *all* of him. I didn't like *all* of him."

"Maybe . . ." Jules's voice was soft. "Maybe I'll just never forgive him for handing me off to Blue. No matter how hard I try."

"You know why he did it. He had to separate us to save us."

"The curse. I know. Why doesn't *knowing* make stuff hurt less?" Jules made a telescope out of her cupped hands and looked at the moon.

"Maybe I don't see the whole picture."

Jules swiveled the telescope and looked at him. "Maybe nobody does when it comes to parents. Maybe it's all too close up."

"Yeah."

"I know we were all basically raised by wolves, but compared to Alfie or Mikki, Blue is . . . I mean, at least Mikki loves D. Even Izzy's parents probably cared about her. They just failed at parenthood, right? Blue just didn't . . . care. I made all these excuses, for years and years. The only thing she cares about is making herself into some kind of cult superstar. She'd do things like forget my birthday or not show up somewhere to pick me up when she promised, or whatever it was that meant I was just intruding on her life . . . and she'd just say, 'I don't brake for feelings,' or 'Crying is for losers.' Basically she let me know, every day, in every way, she was always the most important person in the room. I can't believe Alfie picked her to raise me."

"He didn't have much choice," March said. Jules shot him a look, and he knew what it meant.

He was making excuses again.

They regarded the stars for a moment. They looked like dust.

"Should we go through all the things that can go wrong?" Jules asked.

"Too many to count at the moment," March said. "Which one is the North Star?"

"No idea."

"We should know. What if we get lost?"

"We have GPS." Jules nudged him with her bare foot. "If not, we'll be lost together."

33

JUST PULL TOGETHER

The two-seater kayaks were delivered and dumped on the lawn. Izzy read aloud from a HOW TO KAYAK SAFELY guide. None of them had any experience on the water except for Jules, who had once rowed around a lake.

"It doesn't seem that hard," Izzy said, looking over the brochure. "You just have to pull together."

Mikki eyed the boats with a skeptical glance. "I don't like boats. You got life preservers?"

"Comes with the boats," March assured her.

Dimmy happily agreed to drive them to the beach. "Of course kayaks fit in back!" he said. "Big American truck fits everything! Tonight, we celebrate! Barbecue!"

"Hate to break this up, but we've gotta fly," Darius said, glowering.

"Go ahead now. Be careful and wear those life preservers and don't swim if you eat something!" Mikki waved at them energetically.

Dimmy drove slowly and carefully, tapping his fingers along with the radio. "Your mother is like a dream to me," he told Darius. "So lucky to have crashed into her."

"Yeah," Darius said. "And if you hurt her heart, I break your face."

"Ha-ha, American joke!"

"Not really."

Dimmy dropped them off in the parking lot. "Now I go take your mother to pick up beautiful T-bird car," he said.

"It's ready to zoom-ba. Call when you want pickup." Dimmy waved. "So nice to be part of this beautiful family!"

"You see what I mean?" Darius grumbled. "He's pushy."

They changed in the beach bathroom into identical outfits of white polos, white shorts, white socks, and sneakers. They pulled on sun visors. It was the one photo Izzy had managed to pull off the web, when the Wild Duck Golf Club had hosted a charity tournament. It was clear that all the help, including the caddies, wore a basic uniform.

Izzy settled into the kayak, and Darius pushed it off, then hopped in behind her.

"Not bad for a city boy. Hand me the oar, Iz."

"It's called a paddle," Izzy said.

"Oh, right. I remember that from when I rowed crew at Harvard."

"That's called an oar."

March placed his backpack carefully in the kayak and stepped in gingerly. Jules pushed them off and scrambled into her seat. The kayak wobbled alarmingly, but Jules grabbed the paddle with a show of confidence. "We can do this. How hard can it be?"

She dug her paddle into the water, and the kayak whirled in a circle.

"Uh, Jules? We're supposed to go forward," March pointed out.

"I'll get the hang of it," Jules said as they slid sideways and began to drift back toward the beach.

Somehow, while Izzy instructed them (left, right, left, right), they managed to get the two kayaks to cut through the water. March had studied a website about kayaking in Miami waterways and had memorized the landmarks he needed to know. They found the turning into the river easily.

Soon the golf club loomed ahead, all lush green grass and gentle hills.

They pulled the kayaks up, scraping over roots and trees. They covered the kayaks with a few branches of brush and climbed a steep slope onto the green.

"Just remember," March said. "Look busy. Act like you've got someplace to go." Everyone nodded. "D? Remember, your mark's name is Ann Calloway."

Darius pressed his lips together. "I know my mark."

"And call in a quiet place, so it sounds like you're in an office."

"I'll try not to be *stupid*, okay?"

There was a pause that March felt too raw and edgy to fill. "All right. See you in fifteen minutes."

March struck out across the course. His face felt hot, and not because of the humidity. He had to push it all away. He had to focus. It all depended on him now. If he didn't get into the club, they'd have to cancel the plan and think of something else. The chances of there actually being another way to get at the stone weren't good. This was their best shot.

Shake off the nerves.

I get it, Pop. But how do you shake off nerves when they've got their claws in your skull?

34

SUPER SPORTS MOMS
OF MIAMI

March trotted briskly down the curving walk. He had counted on the fact that the golf club was big and exclusive, and that meant there would be plenty of employees, all dressed just like him. *There's always a new guy*, Alfie used to say. Every time he passed someone in white shorts and a white polo, he gave what he thought of as The Smile, a quick grin that said, *Hiya, I'm a great guy, but I'm super busy.*

The main clubhouse was ahead, a golden Spanish-style McMansion with a circular drive in front. Magenta bougainvillea bloomed, and the grass was a chemical green, so bright it hurt.

He oriented himself from the satellite map in his head. On his left was the blue glint of the pool. It was deserted except for Trini Abbo, who was swimming laps. Izzy had come through! March didn't break stride, but he let out the breath he'd been holding. He felt the fizz and the pop of a job kicking into gear.

Two bodyguards sat at a small table, reading the paper and sweating in their suits.

March crossed to the main entrance. The cool blast of air felt good against his face. He had to figure out where the spa entrance was, and quickly. He didn't want to look like he was lost. He struck out across the lobby with an air of purpose.

As soon as he glimpsed the sign, he swiveled to the left and pushed through a pair of ornate walnut doors. Straight ahead was a young woman at the reception desk. He gave her The Smile and kept on going.

"Hey, hold on!"

March stopped. He turned slowly as pinpricks of nerves danced on his scalp.

"You don't have your ID card."

"It's my first day. Mr. Darwin said to check at personnel, but Marie didn't have one yet."

The woman gave a shrug. "Typical. You'll need it to get through the spa doors. Here." She held out a plastic card on a beaded necklace. "Just keep a guest card until they come through."

March grabbed it and hung it around his neck. "Great. Thanks. I'm Matt."

"Kelly. Welcome to the most beautiful and exclusive golf club in Miami." She rolled her eyes. "We're supposed to say that."

"Got it." March headed for the door, exhaling slowly. He held the key card up to the pad and heard the lock disengage.

He hurried down a long corridor. Most of the doors had discreet labels: MASSAGE ROOM. LOCKER ROOM. TREATMENT ROOM. At the end of the corridor were double doors with frosted glass. Etched on it was JUICE BAR.

He pushed open the door. It was a small room painted in a soft shade of peach. A long counter was against a wall, and a guy in white shorts stood behind it, pouring strawberries into a blender. About ten small round metal tables with bright turquoise chairs dotted the room. Two potted trees flanked double doors that led out to the pool. Plants lined a wide windowsill. Perfect. March placed his backpack next to them.

"Hey," March said as the guy turned. "I'm Matt. It's my first day."

"Didn't hear you were coming. Typical. Sandro. It's slow right now, but it'll pick up when the Pilates class is over. It's about time they sent somebody to help out."

"I'm supposed to water the plants."

"Go for it." Sandro waved a hand at a narrow door. March opened it and found a watering can. He filled it at the utility sink behind the counter, then crossed to the plants.

Sandro's back was turned as he chopped fruit. March lifted the backpack and checked the big plastic soda bottles he'd left by Mikki's garbage. He'd cut off the tops and inverted them into the bottles after he'd put a big dollop of jam on the bottom and a screen on top.

The flies were thick in the bottles, buzzing and batting angrily against the plastic.

He placed them inside the planters and wedged them carefully amid the leafy plants.

Izzy and Jules should already be at the gate. Along with, he hoped, every aspiring model in Miami, thanks to their ad on several online sites.

CASTING OPEN CALL

Teens/Tweens. Male or Female | Age: 12–15. | Role Type: Background, Main. Teens/tweens and Moms wanted for new Miami-based reality series, SUPER SPORTS MOMS OF MIAMI. Teenagers must wear white polo, white shorts, white visor, white sneakers. Background casting plus auditions for main roles. Moms must wear golf or tennis gear. Wild Duck Golf Club, 201 North Marsh Drive. NO CALLS OR EMAILS WILL BE ACCEPTED.

It was the orange vest scheme, but in white this time.

"Hey, Sandro, I've got to stack the pool towels," March called. "I'll be back!"

Sandro waved him off. March pushed open the exterior door, which closed behind him with a soft click. Trini was still swimming laps. He hurried down the slate walkway underneath the royal palms, then cut across the lawn toward the driveway.

As he drew closer to the entrance, he began to hear the static of high-pitched angry conversation. A horn honked with three impatient bleats.

March turned the corner. A line of at least fifty cars trailed from the guardhouse down the lane. More were turning onto the road. Some of the teens and moms had exited the cars and were marching toward the entrance. It was even better than he'd expected! An army of tween and teen models in white shorts and white polos.

March spotted Izzy and Jules at the guardhouse. Right on time. The guard had the phone pressed to his ear.

"Hi, I'm Matt — Ann Calloway sent me from Peterson's office. What's going on?" he asked the guard.

"I've been trying to call up there! It keeps going to voice mail!"

Of course he couldn't get through. Because Darius, using his deepest, smoothest voice, was talking to her as a PGA representative about holding a major tournament at the club. They'd guessed that a professional golf association would never be put on hold.

"My mom just wants to know where to park!" Jules said. "I've got an audition for a shampoo commercial at noon." She rapped the counter. "Time is money!"

"And I need to go to the bathroom," Izzy said. "You *said* to come to this entrance at ten a.m., and I'm on time!"

"I can't *believe* this!" Jules complained. "Let us in, immediately!"

The girls were doing a great Loutsenheizer impression.

"Ann said to just let them in," March murmured. "We don't want to make a scene."

"Buddy, it already *is* a scene!"

One of the moms ran up. "Can you get a move on? It's hot out here. Brianna is sweating!"

Another mom jumped forward. "If you think you're going to jump the line —"

"I'm not jumping the line. I'm just trying to get in!"

"Look, my daughter is Miss Teen Queen of Davie, so —"

"Oh, so she gets special treatment for a lousy beauty contest?"

"Lousy!"

"She's right, though," Jules said. "I'm a top model in Miami, and I've never been treated like this!"

The pushy mom looked Jules up and down while her daughter tugged at her arm. "Mom!"

"Brianna, don't tug!" Then she spoke in a whisper. "If she's a top model, you're Miss America."

March leaned over to the guard. "You'd better just raise the gate, sir."

"Sure," the guard said, pressing the button. "Anything to stop the madness."

The gate rose, and the cars began to pour through. March, Jules, and Izzy hurried toward the clubhouse. By the time they reached it, cars began to flood the circular drive and park. Teenagers — boys and girls in spotless tennis and golf gear — spilled out.

Diversion was a beautiful sight.

"We've got four minutes before Trini leaves that pool," March said. "The clock is ticking. Let the games begin."

35

FLIES, FLIES, FLIES

The group seemed to move in one giant white blob toward the main building. Some of the teens quickened their steps, almost running to get ahead of the pack.

A perplexed man in a suit came forward. "May I . . ."

"Mr. Darwin? Hi, I'm Matt. I'm new. Ann sent me down to see you," March said in a hurried voice. "There's a couple hundred teenagers and moms coming for a photo shoot. More arriving all the time."

"I didn't hear about this!"

"I guess call Ann, but there's a guy with a clipboard outside directing the whole thing. Maybe he can shut the thing down."

Not likely. It was Darius. He was there to create more confusion, putting people on lists, giving false information, and urging everyone to just be calm . . . and hope it had the opposite effect. The virtue of Darius's height and build was that it made him look older. If you added a visor and sunglasses, he might pass for nineteen or twenty.

The man glanced out the window. "Oh . . . my . . . they're going through the flower bed!"

"I know, it's kinda out of control."

"Call Leo in security and tell him to get down here!"

"Right away, sir."

"They can't come in here!" The man ran forward as the models surged into the building.

March, Izzy, and Jules reversed and hurried away. March led them quickly toward the spa. He burst through the double doors to reception.

"Hey, Kelly. It's crazy out there. Did you hear about the film shoot?"

Kelly tossed her ponytail behind her shoulder. "Film shoot?"

"For some reality TV show about athletes. They're casting extras and main roles, I hear. Well, I promised Sandro I'd give him a hand in the juice bar, so . . ."

"They're casting?"

"They especially want blondes."

"Really?"

"Hey, I can sit here for a while if you want to check it out. Sandro said he doesn't need me yet."

"I really can't leave."

"Sure, you can. I'll cover for you. The casting director is out front. He's the one with the clipboard."

Using her phone as a mirror, she smoothed gloss on her lips. "If you really don't mind . . . I'll be right back."

As soon as she pushed through the doors, Izzy and Jules raced in. They followed March into the corridor leading to the treatment rooms. March paused to swipe the door marked SUPPLIES. He grabbed a couple of terry-cloth robes and tossed them to Izzy and Jules. They slipped into them as they ran.

In the juice bar, women sat at the small round tables, sipping at brilliantly colored juices. Izzy and Jules sauntered toward the counter.

"Mother said to order her orange juice, but don't you think she should drink kelp?" Jules asked Sandro.

March crossed to the planters. Quickly he unscrewed the jars. The flies had been buzzing angrily, beating against the plastic. Now they rose, a blizzard of angry, humming insects. To be let loose in a juice bar was probably their idea of fly heaven.

He swatted one fly away as he grabbed a rag off the counter and began to clean the counter. Or pretend to. Izzy and Jules turned away with their juice, choosing a table near the plants.

Sandro glanced over and saw Trini heading for the double doors. "Just in time," he muttered under his breath. "Here comes Medusa."

Trini swept through the door in a terry-cloth robe, a towel wrapped around her hair. "I'll have the usual, Carlos," she said to Sandro. "And I like it really blended."

"I know, Miss Abbo," Sandro said. "And it's Sandro."

"And ice cold. You never make it cold enough. Add more ice. Do I have to make it myself?"

"Yes, ma'am. No, ma'am," he said through gritted teeth.

"Bring it to the table." Trini brushed at a fly as she took her seat. She examined her nails, then consulted her phone. March glanced at the sapphire in the necklace. The gold chain was slender. Easy to snip. He had Hamish's tool in his pocket.

"I'll take it to her," March told Sandro.

"Watch your head. She can bite it off," he muttered.

Trini swatted a fly as he placed the smoothie in front of her. "It's about time."

Jules swatted at a fly again. "This is disgusting!" she said loudly. "What's with all these flies?"

"Ewww," Izzy chimed in.

"I think it bit me!" another woman said, leaping up. Her companion waved the air with a magazine.

Freed from their bottles now, the flies buzzed around the room, sugar-crazy and dive-bombing the fruity drinks.

"You! Do something!" Trini said to March.

"Of course!" March grabbed a rag and began to snap it in the air. He moved closer to Trini. The towel turban fell off her head, and a fly buzzed her ear. She jumped. "Is that a bee? Are they bees? I'm allergic!" Her voice rose higher, and March saw the bodyguards outside stir and begin to crane their necks. One of them rose and started toward the door.

He definitely, positively did not want them in here.

March continued to fan the air, and Izzy backed up, wildly swatting at a fly. She hit Trini on the arm, who screamed again.

"I'm so sorry! It was an accident!"

Jules moved forward, and pushed Izzy toward Trini. "My sister is so sorry!"

"Here's your, uh, turban." Izzy picked up the towel turban and tried to place it back on Trini's head.

Meanwhile March moved closer. "Let me help." With one snip the necklace slipped off into his hand. He shoved it in a pocket.

Jules waved a fly away and knocked over the smoothie. Pulverized kale and apple juice spilled all over Trini's robe.

"You *idiot*!" she screamed. "Carlos! Help me!"

Izzy faded toward the door. Murmuring apologies, Jules followed Izzy outside as Sandro rushed toward Trini. March hurried out after Jules and Izzy.

At spa reception, he dived behind the empty desk and removed Hamish's tool from his pocket. He carefully bent back the prongs on the necklace. It would be faster to just take off, but the longer it looked like Trini had merely lost the necklace, the more time they would have. He pulled the sapphire free and shoved it into his pocket. Izzy had sewed protective Velcro on it, and he made sure it was secure. No mistakes this time.

They ran out the double doors. March dropped the necklace in a corner. Such a waste of diamonds, but it couldn't be helped. He dropped the fake blue gem Hamish had given him a few feet away from the necklace. For a while, Trini might believe that the stone had just rolled away. It was important to buy time.

As they approached the wide walnut front doors, they burst open. Terrence Abbo strode in, surrounded by four beefy bodyguards. March saw the telltale bulge of serious weaponry. Terrence looked as though annoyance would tip over into fury at any random second. He brandished a golf club high in the air, as if looking to bring it down on someone's head.

His eyes swept the reception area and focused on March. He pointed the club at him.

"You! Boy! Find my wife!"

36

GETAWAY

"Go," March murmured to Jules and Izzy. "I'll catch up."

Terrence Abbo wasn't tall, but he made up for it by packing terror into every inch. Something about the opaque darkness of his eyes sucked March into a paralyzing world of doom.

"What is going on out there? This is supposed to be an exclusive club!"

"So sorry, Mr. Abbo, there's a film shoot apparently," March said.

"My wife is supposed to be outside, where all those young people in shorts are standing. This is unacceptable. The car is waiting."

"Let me get the manager for you."

Abbo took a step closer. The scent of grass and aftershave was overpowering. "No manager. Get me my wife! Now! What is your name?" He peered at March closer as the sound of a scream came to them from the direction of the spa. "What was that?"

It was most likely Trini Abbo discovering her necklace was gone, but it was probably better not to mention it.

"Pilates," March blurted. "Very competitive! I'll find your wife, sir!"

March dashed away in the direction of the spa, but instead he swerved and dived down a side corridor, his hands shaking. He found a door and pushed it open, gulping the humid air. He ran down the shaded path toward the front.

He spotted Darius right away, tall and glorious in his tennis whites, his dreads held back with a terry-cloth elastic. Jules and Izzy stood next to him. "See the guys over there next to the guy screaming into his phone? Security," Darius murmured.

"We just ran out of time. Abbo's on the warpath. We need to get out of here. But we need cover."

"On it." Darius moved away, heading for Loutsenheizer Mom.

"I'm just giving you a tip, because you were so nice," Darius said, leaning in. "The casting director is seeing people at the fourteenth hole. Haven't announced it yet. Don't tell anyone, okay?"

"That's a long walk. Brianna's hair will frizz."

"Mom!"

"Golf carts are over there."

Loutsenheizer Mom nudged her daughter, then grabbed her arm. She wiggled through the squirming, selfie-taking crowd, heading for the golf carts.

"Hey, where is she *going*?" Jules asked in a loud voice.

Heads swiveled. Moms grabbed daughters. Soon the edge of the crowd began to move. If the crowd headed to the fourteenth hole, they'd have cover to dive for the kayaks.

"Look, they're leaving!" Jules yelled. "They know where the director is!"

The entire group began to race toward the golf carts. Terrence Abbo burst out of the front door. "STOP, EVERYONE! THERE'S A THIEF HERE!"

No one paid attention. Abbo made a beeline for security.

Darius ran ahead and managed to wrestle a cart away from a mom with a gentle "Sorry, this one's mine." March, Jules, and Izzy piled in.

The golf carts took off like a battalion of tanks. Darius pushed the pedal to the floor, but there was only so fast a golf cart could go. Still, the confusion helped them, and Darius peeled away from the others and struck out across the green.

"Anybody behind us?" he yelled to Izzy.

"Everybody!" Izzy shouted.

"GET BACK HERE!" someone screamed in a megaphone. "CADDIES! SECURITY! CATCH THOSE CARTS!"

When they reached the fourteenth hole, a clutch of startled golfers watched as the teenage boys and girls spilled out of carts and began fixing their hair.

"Let's make a break for it," March said. "Darius, try not to look conspicuous."

"I'm a six-two African American on a golf course, Marcello. How inconspicuous can I be?"

They skirted the crowd, then made a crazy dash for the trees a few yards away. The shade was a relief, and they glanced back. No one had seen them. But a golfer was squinting, looking toward them.

"He's looking for us," Jules said.

"No, he's looking for his ball," March said. He leaned over and picked up a golf ball, then tossed it toward the green. The toss went wild, looping high in a perfect arc and bonking the golfer on the head. They heard his muffled cry.

"Hey!" He and his partner started toward the trees.

"Playing catch was not on Alfie's list of father-son bonding activities," March said.

As the golfers bounded toward them, they tumbled down the bank and scrambled for the kayaks. They pushed off from the bank, paddling in sync now, more used to the rhythm. Within moments they had spun out into the middle of the river and caught the current.

March found his breath. He had a sapphire in his pocket and a clear line to freedom.

"Good job, guys," he said.

"Don't jinx it," Izzy said.

The river twisted, and ahead they caught the glimpse of turquoise bay. From there it would be a straight shot back to the beach.

A speedboat was heading across the bay, the spray a plume of white foam. "That boat is going too fast," Izzy said.

"Jerks," Jules said. "Way over the speed limit."

They shot out into the bay, and the boat turned.

"What's that guy holding?" Jules asked, squinting at a figure on the bow.

"It's some kind of rifle!" Darius exclaimed, just as a spear came flashing through the blue sky and slammed into the kayak.

37

THE TOP CATS RETURN

"We've got to get to shore!" March yelled to the gang, but they would never outrun a speedboat, and he knew it. He dug into the water with his paddle.

Jules half turned. "Who is it? One of Abbo's men?"

March squinted across the water at the two men standing on the bow. Both of them were dark-haired and wore dark sunglasses and dark jeans. He couldn't quite see the captain, who stood in the wheelhouse in shadow.

"I can't tell!"

"I think I recognize one of them," Darius said. "From Paris. What are they doing in Miami?"

Certainty clanged like an alarm bell. "They're chasing the sapphires."

The boat was bearing down on them now, and they were still hundreds of yards from shore. March's arms were already starting to ache.

"Should we swim for it?" Jules asked.

"I never learned to swim," Izzy said, her voice barely audible. "Remember?"

They exchanged panicked glances. They'd forgotten for a moment that Izzy couldn't swim.

The boat pulled up broadside to them, rocking with the waves. The pilot grabbed a bullhorn. "You know what we want," he said.

March swallowed. He stopped paddling. It was useless anyway. For a moment they just drifted in the current.

"This isn't worth it," he said. "We're going to have to hand them over."

"No, Marcello," Darius said. "We've got a shot."

"No, we're going to *get* shot," March said through his teeth.

The two men climbed into a dinghy. One of them kept the speargun pointed at the kayaks. The other one rowed. March sat quietly, his kayak rocking gently.

"I can dive overboard, then try to flip their boat," Jules said.

"You won't be able to get enough leverage in the water. He'll spear you like a grouper."

"You feel that tide?" Darius asked softly. "It's going out."

"Yeah. Noted."

"Remember on the website, it said when the tide goes out it creates a superstrong current, and you have to be careful or you could get swept into the inlet . . ."

". . . and into the ocean," Izzy said in the same soft tone. "If we can just delay . . ."

Jules nodded. "The inlet is too shallow; no boats can get through it."

"But then we'll be in the *ocean*," March said.

"Let's cross that bridge when we get to it," Jules said.

"I *wish* there was a bridge," March said.

"I can divert them," Darius said. "I'll swim for it. They'll think I have the stone and follow me. You can make it to the inlet."

"No," March said. "You'll never make it to shore."

"I will." Darius's voice was ragged with desperation. "I can make it. At least you'll have the stones."

"D!" Izzy's voice shook. "It's too dangerous."

March saw a group of kayakers spill out from the river

into the bay, following the same route they had taken, moving quickly and expertly. Darius was right — the current was running so swiftly that he could see it, a channel of fast water moving just a few feet away. "Hang on, everybody," he murmured. "We could have a shot."

They stopped talking. The boat was too close. The men weren't any better at rowing than the gang was at paddling. The man shipped the oars and grabbed on to the edge of the kayak. "Give me the sapphire."

"Why should I hand it over, just like that?" March stalled. "How about a little negotiation?" He cast about for anything, anything, to delay them. They were drifting now, closer and closer to the current.

"Excuse me, I am holding a gun," the other man said in an undefinable accent, the kind Alfie would call "fake Bulgarian" because an American wouldn't be able to place it. "Do you think I won't use it? You think I care about kids?"

"You think we care about you?" Jules asked, brandishing the paddle. She thumped it against the boat.

"You better watch it, little girl. You want to be fish food?"

"Hurry!" the captain yelled through the bullhorn.

The kayakers in the channel were clearly more experienced than March and the gang. There were about eight kayaks, and they were heading in at an angle, well north of the beach. They knew they could use the current to help bring them in. Their route would bring them within shouting distance. He waved his paddle at them.

One of them cupped his hands around his mouth. "Need some help getting in? It's a tricky current! The tide's coming in!"

The guy moved the speargun down along his body. "We are good, thanks!" he yelled cheerfully to the kayakers, but his face was rigid when he turned back to them. "Give us the stone. *Now.*"

March held up a stone. He saw the paddle in Jules's hand, her knuckles white with effort. He gave her a slight nod to be ready.

March threw the stone high. At the same moment Jules pushed off with her paddle against the boat, sending it skittering out into the current. The man reached up, dropping the speargun. Torn between the speargun and the gem, he stumbled and fell into the water after the gem. The other guy scrabbled for the speargun.

March and the gang were already off, perfectly in sync, and shot out farther into the current. The kayakers were now between them and the boat.

The captain boomed through the bullhorn, but March couldn't make out the words over the roaring in his ears as he pushed his paddle against the water. It was a race toward the inlet, and the current was their friend.

Paddles digging deep into the water, white water foaming around them, they shot into the inlet. Behind them they heard the cabin cruiser power down, unable to follow. Sneaking a quick look back, March saw the captain staring out at them. He raised a hand like a gun. He used his index finger. And shot.

38

NEXT STOP PORTUGAL

Moments later they flew into a deep green ocean. Current hit current, sending the boats spinning. Choppy waves buffeted the kayaks. To the left they could see heavy surf pounding the ocean beach.

The current was sending them straight out to the deep water.

Izzy's face was white with terror.

"We have to get to the beach!" Jules shouted.

"Put your vests on!" March ordered.

They pulled on the vests. Straining, pushing, grunting, they found their rhythm and positioned the kayaks toward the beach.

The two kayaks rose and fell on the swells. White caps crashed and foamed. The beach seemed impossibly far. The kayaks seemed incredibly flimsy.

"Izzy," Darius said, his voice a croak. He cleared his throat. "I want you to climb back here with me. I'm going to keep my arms around you. You don't let go of my neck. You don't let go. I'm going to keep you safe."

Gingerly, Izzy climbed into the rear seat with Darius while Jules reached over to steady their kayak. Izzy was trembling as she folded herself against Darius and put her arms around his neck. She faced out to sea, and her eyes suddenly widened.

"Guys . . ." Izzy said.

A wall of water was coming at them, larger than any of the swells they'd seen. Even as they watched, it gathered force and power, the top of the wave licked with white foam.

"We've got to ride it in!" March shouted. "HANG ON!"

Izzy let out a shrill scream as the kayaks lifted high, high above the surface of the ocean. The people on the beach looked as small as dolls.

"Oh, oh, oh, NOOOOOOOOO!"

The tremendous energy of the surf picked up the kayaks and hurtled them toward shore. Screaming, they could do nothing but hang on. March's paddle flew into midair as the energy of the wave rushed them headlong forward. The power of it sent them rocketing into space, green water all around them.

A few terrifying seconds later March felt the kayak scrape against the sand. He felt the suck of the tide trying to drag him out again, and he quickly scrambled out, falling in the water, stumbling, rising, falling, and dragging himself and the kayak in, Jules by his side. He wiped his eyes free of the stinging salt water.

Izzy was lying on the sand, her hair wet, coughing, trying to get up. Darius bent over her. Murmuring, he picked her up and set her on her feet. He turned toward March, and the expression on his face made March's heart skip a beat. He'd never seen Darius look so afraid.

"Whoa, dude." A young man in board shorts approached them. "That was, like, a suicide run. Awesome." He held out a fist to bump against March's.

Weakly, March lifted a shaking fist. "Awesome."

39

LEGACIES

"You don't understand, Hamish," Jules said. "The guy had a speargun. And he was prepared to use it."

"Closest escape ever," March said. "Mostly luck we're standing here."

"And the wave," Izzy said. "It was the size of a mountain."

Darius said nothing. He leaned against the wall, looking out Hamish's window.

"The Top Cats gang wasn't after the diamonds in Paris," March said. "They were after the sapphire. This was no coincidence. Did you know about this?"

"Of course not," Hamish said. "But am I surprised? Look, young yogis, these are the most expensive sapphires in the history of gems. So if my tipster happened to tip off someone else . . . how was I to know? It's just . . . uh, unfortunate that the most infamous gang in Europe has decided to cross the ocean at this particular time and intersect with you."

"Intersect?" Jules spit out. "They had a *speargun!*"

"And they *must* have known we were there," March said.

"I'm guessing that they were already staking out the club," Hamish said. "They radioed the boat and said, 'Hey, the game is afoot. Stop those kayaks.'"

"And we've really crossed them now," March said. "They know we have two."

"Indeed. What did you throw at them anyway?"

"One of the cheap blue zirconias you gave me," March said.

"Just like Alfie always said: 'It never hurts to have a spare.' So it's all good," Hamish said. He held up a hand as they opened their mouths to protest. "True, it's more dangerous than we wanted or expected. But." He spread out his hands. "We have two stones. Only one more to go. Do we have a choice but to go on?"

"We always have a choice," Jules said.

"Who's the next mark?" March asked.

Hamish picked up his phone and adjusted his reading glasses. He tapped in some information, then looked over the top of his glasses at them. "Have you heard about a pop star person called Lemon?"

"Lemon Cartelle?" Jules shook her head. "Hamish, you'd have to be living under a rock not to have heard of Lemon. Haven't you heard 'Devoted 2 U 4 Only 1 Nite'? Or 'You Love Me You Know It Uh-Huh'? She's had about five top-ten hits in a row."

"Jules, my young friend, you are talking to an old person," Hamish said. "I'm still pissed that the Eagles broke up."

"She's your easy mark?" March asked. "You're crazy. She's got to be surrounded by bodyguards and paparazzi."

"Ah! This is most likely true," Hamish agreed. "But may I remind you that you just stole a gem from a much harder target? She's just bought a condo in Brooklyn, territory you know well, and where your safe house is. I mean, the one I found for you. Cakewalk."

"What exactly is a cakewalk anyway?" Jules asked.

"Duck soup," Hamish answered.

"Well, that explains it," March said.

Hamish leaned back, a look of astonishment on his face. "All this resistance! All of you in this room are the children of some of the best criminals ever to walk the earth. Where's your pride?" He pointed at March and Jules. "Son and daughter of Alfie McQuin, you have the two most famous sapphires in the world in your grasp. How can you possibly turn down the third? Considering your genetic imprint?"

"I'm not my father," March said.

"Of course you are! You've got his eyes, his hands, and his marvelous capacity for breaking and entering." Hamish put his hands together. "We're so close. If we tried to sell these two, we'd have the feds on us in a New Jersey minute, which is faster than New York — have you seen the way they drive? I'd have to cut them down, and then we'd just have a handful of little blue gems. Our only shot is with Ransome. So. Do this one thing. Check out the mark. If there is *one iota* of an insurmountable problem, then I recut the gems and hope we get enough to live for a couple of years, and hope that Zillah takes pity on us. But don't forget — the stones *want* to be reunited. The sooner we do that and hand them off, the better for all of us."

March felt the lure. Only one heist to go. The make-or-break moment that sang in his blood.

The stones felt heavy in his pocket. But they didn't weigh as much as where he came from, and who he was.

40

THIS CURSE IS SERIOUS

That night, they walked to the beach close to Mikki's house. They trudged along the sand, then plopped down to watch the slow progress of an orange sun through a powder-blue sky. Streaks of pink and purple began to spread along the horizon, and the sky turned lilac.

"Only one left," March said. "Hamish has a point. And it's in Brooklyn, basically our home ground. That's a plus."

"So you want to do it?" Jules asked.

"I want to go to New York and check out the mark, yeah," March said. "We've got two of the most famous sapphires in the world. How can we walk away?"

"I almost lost Izzy in that surf," Darius said. He turned to her. "I almost *lost you*."

She put a hand on his knee. "You didn't, though."

"It felt like someone wanted to *wrench* you from my arms," Darius said. "This curse is serious. The whole thing feels too big."

Nobody spoke. The sun was blood orange now, right at the horizon line. In just seconds it would wink fire, and then be gone. The hot wind picked up, blowing sand in their faces. Maybe it would rain.

"Okay," Jules said with sudden briskness. "I get it. The curse is bad, Hamish could be lying, the Top Cats are scary, the feds know who we are. All bad. Plus we're retired, and today I almost puked when I saw that wave. But we have tickets back to New York tomorrow. We'll go, we'll check out the mark, and we'll take a vote there."

"The important thing is to stick together." Izzy tugged on the sleeve of Darius's T-shirt. "Right?"

Darius dug his bare feet in the sand. He looked out at the sea. The water had turned a dark gray, stained with red.

"I'm not going with you," he said.

41

FEALTY FLIES

Izzy pressed her hands against her mouth. Her brown eyes were huge, and her gaze didn't leave Darius's face. He didn't look at her.

He couldn't look at her, March knew.

He couldn't look at any of them.

"It's just too hard to be with you right now," Darius said.

Jules shot March a look. *Say something.*

What could he say? He couldn't say, *I'm not mad*, because he still *was*.

All he knew was that he felt awful. Scraped raw. Confused. Like he wanted to dig a hole in the sand and crawl into it like a turtle.

"Look," March started. "I think that —"

"I messed up royally," Darius interrupted. "Stupid like my dad. Careless like my mom. Whenever I get something good, I lose it. That's *my* genetic imprint."

"Not so," Izzy said, her voice soft. "You haven't lost anything."

Can we review that? March wanted to say, but Jules was pressing his foot so hard he thought he might whimper.

"You don't trust me anymore," Darius said to March. "Today, you kept reminding me what to do. You never used to do that."

"I just wanted everything to work," March said. "The stakes were big."

"You didn't rag at Jules, or Izzy."

"Do you want an apology?"

Darius shook his head. "March, I don't want anything except to go back to that day in the bank, and this time I just walk away."

March felt his breath catch. It was what Darius had called him. *March.* He never called him by his name. He called him Marcello, or Marco, or bro, or dude. In Darius's mouth, suddenly his own name sounded terrible. Serious.

Like a good-bye.

"It's just . . . too hard to be with you right now," Darius continued. "All of you," he added, with a gentle hand on Izzy's knee. "Looking at you is painful. Knowing what I did to you."

"D, we don't care," Jules said.

"Appreciate that, Jules, but I *do*." He straightened and shook his head. "Anyway, I should stick around here. Watch over my mom. Don't have a good feeling about what's going on." He held up a hand. "I know what you're going to say, and you're right. She was never there for me. Ever. She lies like it's nothing. Went to jail three times, and I bounced into the system. Got beat up, got betrayed, got kicked out of school. So tell me something. Why do I feel guilty?"

Izzy tried to smile. "Because you're sweet as coconut pie."

Darius dug his bare feet deeper into the sand. "I just got to do something right, for once. So I'm staying."

Jules and Izzy turned to March, their eyes pleading. Like he could stop this. Like he could come up with some combination of words that would change Darius's mind. When all March could think about was keeping them on track, getting them the funds to remake a life, recapture a dream.

"We'll miss you," March said. He was going to add something about Darius coming back to them, but Izzy suddenly jumped to her feet. She took off down the beach, running fast, not looking back.

Darius gave a sigh so deep his shoulders shuddered. He got up and walked away in the opposite direction.

And just like that, they were broken.

42

SOME GOOD-BYES ARE
WORSE THAN AWFUL

The next morning, Izzy kept her head down and leaned against Darius to say good-bye.

"I'm so sorry, Iz," he murmured, his head bent over her, as though he were cradling her in his body. She looked so tiny next to him. "This isn't forever. It's just now."

She nodded, her head against his arm.

"And if you need me, I'll come to you, no matter where you are."

She nodded again.

March watched Izzy. She was folded up like a leaf. She took a deep breath, and then it was like she gathered herself together from the ground up, like a tree.

She pulled away and smiled at Darius. She nodded again, a gesture of understanding.

She walked out the door to Hamish's car. He would drive to the airport and leave his car in long-term parking, then hop a different flight to New Jersey. They'd meet in Brooklyn that afternoon.

"I'm going to worry about her no matter what," Darius said. "You take care of her for me, both of you? She's strong, she's fine, but she needs to know someone is there."

"Absolutely," Jules said.

"I'm there," March said.

"I messed up," Darius said. "I put us in a place that's bad. You get us out, you hear me? You can do it."

March bumped fists with Darius. His throat was thick, and he couldn't say good-bye. He didn't know how the impossible had happened; he only knew his world had blown apart.

He walked out into the bright sunshine, not really sure if he'd see his friend again. From everything he knew, everything he'd seen, life was like that.

Jules didn't speak. She kept her head turned, her face toward the window.

He leaned closer. "That was worse than awful."

"Then why didn't you *say anything*?"

"I tried!"

"We'll *miss you*? That's the best you could do?"

"He'd already made up his mind. Besides, he wants to take care of Mikki."

She turned. Sometimes Jules's gray eyes were so clear, it was like he could see right through their light into the truth. "Do you really think he would have stayed," she said, "if he hadn't felt so ashamed that he let you down?"

43

IMMA POP STAR

They met Hamish in Brooklyn. He showed up in a white panel truck with SCRUMPTIOUS BAKERY: WE BAKE IT YOU EAT IT on the side.

"One of my nephews owns it," Hamish explained, waving at the bakery truck. "He's an idiot, but he comes in handy. I'm taking you to his garage. That's your safe house. But first, I thought we'd just do a drive-by of Lemon's condo — fancy building in Williamsburg. We've got no time to lose. No time to be sad. The game is afoot!"

Hamish snaked through Brooklyn traffic. Beyond the windows, street life was humming in a riot of dogs, strollers, beards, bicycles, and shops selling beeswax and handmade brooms. Every chair in the sidewalk cafés in Williamsburg was filled with young people enjoying sunshine and green tea. March had walked these streets many times, but he'd been retired. Now that he was in the game again, he was noticing things, like how the lights were timed, if there were cops on the street, what kind of locks were on the many bicycles.

Lemon lived in a luxury building that was pretending to look like a warehouse. Hamish pulled over into an illegal space, and the gang tumbled out.

"Doing this just seems kind of . . . *lesser* without Darius," Izzy said.

"I know," Jules said.

March did, too, but he couldn't say it. He checked out

the security as they strolled across the street. The three of them traded notes.

"Security cameras. Doorman."

"Plus a desk guy."

"After hours they buzz you in."

"Parking garage with key card. Two attendants on duty."

"The alley has a double-reinforced metal gate with security key-card lock."

"Not to mention a squad of paparazzi and fans hanging out in front of the building."

"Roof?" March asked Jules.

"Looks to me like cameras up there, too," Jules said, her eyes moving over it. "Some kind of sitting area up there, maybe a pool. Plus there's no access from a nearby building."

Izzy slowed down. "There she is. Wow."

Lemon Cartelle stepped out of the building, straight toward the photographers. Her short spiky hair was like a splotch of fluorescent yellow from a toddler's paint box. She wore pink leggings and a green hoodie that said IMMA POP STAR on the front and YOU'RE NOT on the back. March lifted his phone, pretending to take a photo, and zoomed in.

She was wearing the Midnight Star. It nestled right between her collarbones. She smiled and posed for the cameras, holding up a bottle of fluorescent yellow PowerU drink. A yellow Mini Cooper waited at the curb while Lemon posed. The whole scene seemed staged: the pops of color — lemon yellow, bright green, hot pink — against the pale stone of the fancy building.

She waved at the photographers, then climbed into the passenger seat. A driver was behind the wheel. The windows of the car were tinted, and they couldn't tell anything more.

March hurried back to the truck, Jules and Izzy at his heels. He swung inside. "Let's follow her."

Startled, Hamish froze. "What? I'm not a *wheelman*!"

"Just drive!"

44

MINDFUL PEOPLE

Hamish hit the gas, and the truck lurched into a pothole. He ground the gears, and they roared after the Mini.

"This is crazy!" Hamish yelled, running through the last millisecond of a yellow light. "I'm driving like a maniac!"

"This is Brooklyn," March said, leaning forward. "Everyone drives like a maniac."

The yellow Mini scampered through traffic, and Hamish did his best to keep it in sight. He screeched to a halt at a red light just in time to avoid a tall redheaded mom pushing a stroller. She glared at him.

"Lovely little boy!" Hamish shouted in apology.

"We lost them," Izzy said.

March pushed open the door. "I'll try to keep them in sight." He jumped out of the truck, and Jules leaped out after him. They ran around the corner and squinted through the traffic. The yellow Mini was gone.

"There!" Jules pointed. The Mini was disappearing into a parking lot, and a small figure in a baseball cap was hurrying toward the side entrance of a building.

Jules texted Hamish as they ran down the block.

"It's a gym," March said, indicating a discreet sign on the building.

BREATHE

FITNESS FOR MINDFUL PEOPLE

"Oh, brother," Jules said.

"No. Oh, Brooklyn."

They pushed open the darkened glass door. They were in a reception area with steel-gray couches and glass tables. It looked more like a hotel than a gym. The pretty young woman at the desk wore a tank top and an annoyed expression when she saw two kids. "Minimum age is eighteen."

March gave her The Smile. *Pour every ounce of charm you got into it. Except not too much, because you've got to look sincere.*

"Hi. Our mom told us to meet her here."

She frowned. Suddenly March missed Darius. He was six feet two inches of handsome, persuasive charm.

"Aren't you supposed to be in, like, school?"

"It's four o'clock," Jules pointed out. "Our mom is in Om Spin," she added, reading the class off a monitor. "We've got her phone. Can we just go in for a minute?"

"She is totally freaking out," March said.

Just then the phone rang. The young woman held up one finger to stop them as she answered it. "Breathe, Fitness for Mindful People . . . Oh, I'm sorry you have a problem. If you'd just hold . . ."

"Can we . . . ?" March asked.

"She is super freaked!" Jules said, shifting from foot to foot.

The woman shook the finger. ". . . I understand you're a founding member, sir, but we don't *have* karaoke yoga . . . I don't need an explanation. I can, like, get the concept from the *name*."

"We'll be right back!" March said, dashing in.

Jules's phone lit up, and she showed it to March.

U in? Izzy texted.

Yessss. Hamish was awesome.

The vast room was crowded with people on machines

and lifting weights. The subdued lighting and electronic music were almost lulling, if you didn't count all the sweating and grunting. A lavender neon light in a corner read STUDIOS.

"This place is huge," March said. "She could be anywhere."

"She used a private entrance, so I'm guessing she has a private room," Jules said. "She probably has a personal trainer."

"Maybe we'll get lucky," March said. "We could snatch the necklace right here. Hard to get to her without a posse around, right?"

"We haven't even decided to *do* this yet," Jules pointed out.

They moved toward the darkened hallway. Jules cocked her head. "Do you hear that?"

All March could hear was thumping bass.

"It's Lemon's hit song. The one from that movie where the world is destroyed and the survivors build cities out of car parts. What's it called? *Demolition*? No — *Dissolution*! And they all have sports teams with these ultimate sport play-off battles . . ."

"Missed that one."

"I went with D. He loved it."

They moved down the hallway, tracking the sound. March stopped in front of a door with a small glass window with a shade over it from inside.

He stood on tiptoes to try to peer inside, Jules right next to him. He had an impression of a large room with high ceilings that disappeared into shadow. He heard Lemon's amplified voice thump in time to the beat. He recognized the song now. It was the one he heard on every radio.

"When all the world's in pieces,

I will find yeewwwwoooo."

"I can't really see," he whispered. "Just a corner of the room. It looks empty . . ."

"Let's go in," Jules whispered. She tried the knob. "It's not locked."

She opened the door a few inches. March peered around her shoulder.

The music boomed at full volume. The space seemed completely empty, but March recognized Lemon's gym bag on the floor.

Then he felt something. Air displaced. Movement.

And Blue dropped down from the ceiling like a spider.

45

NOTHING WORSE THAN FAMILY

Blue flipped off the aerial silks and landed lightly. She smiled, her glittering aqua eyes raking over them. Without her stage makeup, she looked only a little bit more ordinary, a striking woman with taut muscles and an air of challenge.

March felt Jules next to him, suddenly growing small. The energy that always hummed through her body shut down.

They hadn't seen Blue in person in a year. A familiar surge of rage hit him, gathering so fast and hard his vision seemed to fuzz out for a moment.

"Looking for me?" she asked.

"No," March said. "We were just following a rat trail, and you showed up."

Blue clicked her tongue. "You always were a nasty kid."

"How would you know, *Auntie*?"

Blue examined Jules as she wound a length of silk around her hand. "So now the two of you are in the big city. Miss me yet, Jules?"

"I wouldn't miss you for a million years," Jules said.

"Ooooh, snap. The city has made you so hard!"

"No. You did that."

Blue shrugged. "I taught you how to be on your own, because nobody else is going to have your back. That's the best thing I could have given you. But kids always blame who raised them. Nothing worse than family to ruin an afternoon. You mind? I'm working. My client should be here in a minute."

It chilled March to see how Blue could just dismiss Jules that way. Her indifference froze his blood.

"Since when do you train people?" Jules asked.

"I trained you, didn't I? Anyway, Lemon Cartelle isn't an ordinary person. Are you following me, or her? Are you big fans? Do you want her autograph?" She gave a mocking smile.

"She must be paying you a lot," Jules said. "You don't do anything without a payout."

Blue snorted. "Here's a secret. Famous people don't pay for anything. She never picks up a check. That sports drink she's always clutching? She hates it. They just pay her to carry it around. Her movie studio sent over a car the other day that matches her hair. For free! She already has six cars back in LA. Only she can't drive, so I have to drive her everywhere. I'm supposed to be her friend, and I'm a chauffeur."

Blue's mouth turned down. The mask had slipped. There it was, that bitterness March recognized now.

"There's got to be something in it for you," Jules said.

"Oh, Jules." Blue sighed. "Still playing the poor little girl? Even in your fancy town house with the pool? Did you find out that riches don't make you happy? When did we become enemies anyway?"

"When I found out that you only raised me to collect the payouts Alfie sent," Jules spit out.

"Or maybe when you killed our dad," March said.

"Here we go again. Alfie *slipped* that night," Blue said. "You better watch who you accuse of murder, kiddo. And when it comes to Alfie, well . . . if you make your living in high places, there's always a chance you'll fall." She gave a catlike smile, except that would be an insult to cats. "I'm just a little bit better in the air."

The dismissal of Alfie's death, the casual way she said it, made black rage move through March.

"You're after what you can get," Jules said.

Blue laughed. "And you're not? You know what Lemon's got around her neck. So, you decided to follow in your father's footsteps? Even though he didn't have the courage to handle the rocks in the first place?"

March and Jules shot each other confused looks.

"You know Alfie stole the original stones, right?" Blue laughed. "You didn't know! He cracked a safe down in Virginia horse country. Stole 'em from a billionaire — Ransome. Maggie was his partner. Apparently he got spooked and passed them off to her, then took off and left her there with a bagful of loot. She almost got caught — they searched the servants. She hid the stones in a vacuum-cleaner bag." Blue shrugged. "She forgave him . . . she always did. But it wasn't the same. She talked to me about leaving him." Blue leaned in and peered at them. "You two look a little sick. Need to sit down?"

A side door banged open, and Lemon Cartelle entered, chugging on a bottle of water. "Blue, let's get started. I've got to meet my new agent in an hour." Her gaze wandered over to Jules and March. "Oh. Hi. Sorry, kids, I've gotta work. Do you want a selfie?"

"This is my nephew and niece," Blue said. March noted how her face had changed, her expression now warm and open. She reached out to tug at Jules's hair. Jules looked too confused, too numb, to slap her hand away.

"Cool. Nice to meet you," Lemon said. "Hey, do you want a couple of tickets to the KidzPix awards? See your aunt in action with me?"

"They're not allowed to go to concerts," Blue said, her face suddenly tight.

"Sure, we are!" March said. "We're fourteen now!"

"Hold out your phone. I've got the coolest technology." Lemon rummaged in her bag and took out her phone. She touched it to March's. "I just sent you a bar code for two tickets. Just go to the Special Visitors line. Love to hang, but . . ." Her eyes moved to Jules. "Hey, you look just like your aunt. That's so sweet!"

March could almost see the sentence forming in Jules's mouth.

I am nothing like her.

He saw the fear in her eyes. He knew why. He pulled Jules toward the door. They were all afraid. Darius, Izzy, Jules, and him. All afraid they'd gotten the worst of their parents.

Alfie had left their mother with the gems. Left her to take the heat.

46

THE PLACE INSIDE

"Of course I didn't know Alfie stole the stones!" Hamish cried as he drove through Brooklyn. "I never knew. *Nobody* knew. It was the biggest mystery in Crime World!"

"She said that he left Mom there," March said. "Just left her!"

"That doesn't sound like Alfie," Hamish said.

But there was doubt in his voice. March heard it.

Which Alfie? March wondered. The one he remembered, the fun dad? Or the thief he didn't really know?

"Did you know Blue was here?" March asked Hamish. "You'd better tell us everything."

"I might have read something about it."

"Ham!"

"I was going to tell you!" Hamish put up both hands, and the truck swerved and almost hit a parking meter. He jerked it back onto the road. "I know, when it comes to bad karma, Blue is the queen! I just thought maybe that connection could give you an edge. Get you closer to Lemon."

"Or get us competition. We know Blue was a thief before she became some sort of wannabe cult star. She stole ten million in bonds."

Izzy looked up from her tablet. "She was telling the truth about Lemon. They're pals. She's all over Lemon's Instagram account. And there's an article about how they met in LA and have been besties ever since. Typical stupid fluff stuff, but. It looks like some of it is true. Now that she's hanging with the stars, why steal a sapphire?"

"Exactly! This could be good. Now that you have VIP tickets, you could plan the heist around the awards," Hamish suggested. "Maybe you could get backstage."

"Maybe," March said. "Lots could go wrong."

Jules said nothing. She sat in the backseat, her legs drawn up, hugging her knees. The look was on her face again, the look that scared him. Like a dead-bolted door without a key.

They were in deep now. Maybe there was no turning back. The stones in his pocket felt charged, like they had their own magnetic field. They tugged at him, pulling him toward Lemon. He could feel it.

Now that Blue was involved . . . This put his twin in a kind of danger he hadn't expected. It was almost worse than falling off a roof.

It was falling into pain that would never heal.

Being around Blue had brought Jules back to that place she went to. Someplace remote and deep inside. When she'd close the door to her room and play her records and draw and not come out for hours. Lost in sketching her odd landscapes of lilac trees and skies with orbiting planets, and always a black figure in the distance.

He could lose her there.

Suddenly, with an ache in his gut, he understood what Izzy had told him in Florida. About what she feared for Darius. *We could lose him.*

He'd never thought that before. That they could lose one another. Not because of the police, or the feds, or the system, but because of their pasts. Because of *themselves.*

47

TURNAROUND

They left the hipster cafés and shops of Williamsburg behind and drove to a part of Brooklyn March didn't know, with dilapidated warehouses and sagging storefronts, many of them abandoned.

"Ham, are we even *in* Brooklyn anymore?"

"Almost there. Joey got an unbelievable deal on the rent. Then he finds out it floods on a regular basis. Shrewd business move, right? Typical. He uses the space for the stuff he sells, you know, the stuff that fell off a truck."

He pulled into an alley and parked. Then he led them to a side door, fitting the key into a padlock. He pushed open the metal door and flipped on the lights.

Wooden planks and palettes were set out on top of cinder blocks to raise everything off the floor. There were at least fifty beanbag chairs piled in a small mountain. A row of strollers were lined up next to boxes marked TAP SHOES and MATTRESS COVERS.

"Strollers?" March asked. "Mattress covers?"

"I told you he was an idiot," Hamish said. "When you deal in stolen stuff, you're supposed to move flat-screen TVs, stereos, stuff you can sell easily. Who knocks off a truck for *strollers*? Tap shoes? Answer: my nephew. Not the sharpest tool in the shed." He flipped on more lights. The space lit up, the rest of it a vast empty concrete floor, with a makeshift raised room built out of lumber in one corner. "Joey calls it his man cave," Hamish said, waving at it. "Comes here when his wife kicks him out. There's a fridge, some blankets. Just drag some of the beanbags in there."

March noticed Izzy frowning at her phone. "What's wrong?"

"I'm worried about Darius. He says things are weird at Mikki's."

"Weird could mean anything," March said. "It could even mean normal, in our world."

"Sure," Izzy said, unconvinced.

Hamish rubbed his hands together. "The awards are in two days. I'll make myself scarce so you can kick-start some mastermind planning. My advice? Don't fight your karma. It's a losing battle."

The door banged shut behind Hamish.

"Home sweet home," Izzy said, looking around. "It's not so bad."

"If you like mildew," March said. He gave a quick look at Jules, who had settled herself into a beanbag chair. She looked relaxed because everybody looked relaxed in a bean-bag chair, but her fingers were gripping the sheepskin.

"Look, we have to talk about this Lemon heist," he said. "I didn't want to say anything in front of Hamish, but it's not too late to pull out."

"I was thinking the same thing," Izzy said. "I want to get the money for Darius. But the curse . . . things keep coming true! Now Darius is gone. Because of the stones! Fealty flew."

"Look, it's killing me to walk away from fifty million," March said. "Maybe we should just sell what we have and cross our fingers that the curse is done with us."

Jules spoke up from her beanbag mountain. "You're doing this because of me, aren't you?"

"Of course not! I'm just . . ."

Jules slid down and landed on her feet. "You think I can't handle Blue."

"Nobody can handle Blue," Izzy said. "She's scary."

"It's not worth it," March said. "We can't get to Lemon without tangling with her. What if she's after the sapphire, too?"

"All the more reason to do it." Jules's eyes weren't remote now. They shone with anger and certainty. "We can't walk away from this. She killed our father and tried to steal our fortune. We have a chance to get back at her, steal that sapphire right from under her nose. And I think I know how."

48

GHOSTS

"Jules, wait," March said. "I don't think —"

"Just listen!" Jules strode toward them across the space, full of purpose now. "I've been thinking. Blue has been spending money like crazy this past year. She created the website with streaming video. The store with Blue merch. She cut an album and paid for it herself. She promoted her own European tour — London, Milan, Barcelona, Istanbul, Dubrovnik — in big arenas, not illegal pitches . . . and nobody came! It totally makes sense. What if she blew all the money? What if she needed more? She's a thief. Stealing is always her first way out. Believe me, she's after the sapphire, too."

"Okay," March said. "But why is that a good thing? She's got the in. Lemon trusts her. We don't know what she's planning."

"It doesn't matter. Hamish is right — we do it at the concert. If we steal it, and it looks like *she* did it, Lemon will press charges. Sure, Blue won't pay for Alfie, or for the bonds, or for trying to steal the moonstones, but she'll pay for *something*."

"Okay," March said cautiously. "I get what you're saying. But. How?"

"Lemon said it herself." Jules smiled. "I look just like her."

There were plenty of pitfalls in Jules's idea. March shook his head again and again as Jules explained all the reasons she could do it.

"But how will you know the routine?" March asked. "You can't just improvise up in the air!"

Jules set her jaw. "I can figure it out."

March shook his head. "Too dangerous."

They argued until well after midnight and drifted to sleep in their separate beanbags, sleeping hard and deep.

March woke in the gray light and didn't know where he was at first. He had been dreaming, again, of a woman walking, her white gown streaming river water. His fingers felt cold, and he checked his secret pocket for the sapphires. They felt wet.

He sat up, shaken. He'd rolled off the beanbag during the night. The concrete beneath him was damp. Streaky light came through the grated windows.

Hamish had said the place was damp. That's what it was. Not a walking ghost.

The concrete floor was hard and cold. He thought about his soft bed in the town house, how they'd ordered everything online and filled the house with pillows and comforters and sofas and big armchairs and everything that was as cushy and soft as possible, as if they could cushion themselves against their pasts. He remembered last Christmas, when they'd dragged in a fifteen-foot tree and crammed it with ornaments, so many the tree tipped over. How they'd bought one another hoverboards and computers and sneakers and boots and stupid toys and gargantuan chocolate bars. It had been the most fun they'd ever had.

But if you thought about it, it was just a bunch of kids, really, trying to fill a space that couldn't be filled. Fighting ghosts. Thinking that giving toys they never had were weapons against parents who didn't care or that fancy chocolate made up for eating cereal for dinner every night or that a tree with sterling silver ornaments was better than a mom who was constantly in a revolving door marked GO TO JAIL, DO NOT PASS GO.

Or a father who left you in bleak apartments with a wad of cash and a promise to come back. Or left your mother in a tight spot just because he was spooked.

He couldn't blame Darius for wanting to stay with Mikki. He still had a mom who cared.

March had called him stupid. Deliberately. Knowing how much it would hurt.

He was the one who owed an apology.

When you fight so hard to hold on to a home that you lose the people you made it for, you're a chump.

Which made him a chump.

He would text Darius today.

No more sleep was possible. He got up. Maybe he'd slip out now, buy breakfast for everyone. Eggs and bacon on rolls. Hot tea for Jules with three sugars. OJ for Izzy. Coffee with lots of milk for him. He tiptoed out of the makeshift office.

He stopped.

Wet footprints on the concrete floor. As if someone had been there last night, face pressed against the streaked window, staring down at the bodies on the floor.

49

FRACTURED FAMILIES

Izzy had come up behind him without him hearing her.

She looked down at the footprints. "It's Zillah. She was here. I dreamed about her, didn't you?"

"It's just damp."

"You know it's not. Zillah is *here*. And Darius hasn't texted me back. Not for hours."

"He will."

"I'm scared." Izzy leaned against him, the way she used to do with Darius. "My heart is *riven*. Split down the middle. Just like Zillah said."

"I miss him, too. I just think . . . if we could get the last one, it will help Darius *and* Jules. If she could get back at Blue, make her pay . . ."

"Blue can't pay for everything she did to Jules," Izzy said.

"Yeah. I get that. But, Iz, Jules has to *feel* like Blue has. You know?"

Izzy nodded, her curls soft against March's arm. "Okay."

An otherworldly scream echoed across the space. Izzy grabbed his arm. "Zillah!"

Light blinded them. A shadowy shape filled the doorway.

Izzy screamed.

The scream was echoed by the shape in the doorway. "AAAAAAHHHH!"

"EEEEEEEEE!" screamed Izzy.

Jules was there in a flash. "What is it?"

A man walked farther into the space. He pressed his hands against his heart. "WHAT THE . . . You scared the guacamole outta me!"

The door slammed behind him. The squealing scream became rusty hinges, and the ghost was just a youngish man in a sweatshirt.

He put his hands on his hips. "Whoa. I didn't remember anybody was here." He squinted at them. "You must be the kids Hamish said are staying here."

"Good guess," March said.

"Let me ask you something. If somebody puts ketchup on eggs, is that so bad?"

"Um," March said. "What?"

He shoved his hands in his pockets. "I mean, is that grounds for divorce or something? I didn't know the eggs were special and had herbs and stuff. Who puts rosemary in eggs? Is that a thing? My life has gotten so crazy-in-a-bad-way since Heather started watching the Food Network. One minute I'm eating scrambled eggs, and the next thing I know, I'm in the driveway and she's calling me a barbarian and throwing the car keys at me." He thrust his head toward them and pointed to his forehead. "You see that? They *hurt* when they hit your head. I have a *dent*!" He sighed. "I love that woman like a crazy person, but she's got to stop throwing me out. Anyway, I should introduce myself, right? I'm Joey Indiana. Hamish's nephew, if you haven't figured it out."

"March, Izzy, and that's Jules," March said.

Joey looked down at the floor. The wet prints were almost gone, but you could still see the damp outline. "Yeah, it gets damp here. I should, I don't know, do something. Buy a fan? A humidifier? Is that what I mean? Things get moldy, and I can't sell 'em. Anyway, happy to loan you the place. Hamish is such a whack, right? But he's my uncle, and I love him. I know about the big score. I had ahold of one couple a weeks ago, got left with a warehouse full of strollers. Worthless. Might as well give 'em away. Look, if you got room for another guy on this job . . ."

"We'll let you know."

"Sure, whatever." Joey looked disappointed. "So, hope you had a comfy night," he said, peeking past them into the office. "Hamish stayed once when Keiko kicked him out. Said it gave him rheumatism. 'Course, she won't kick him out again, seeing that she left him."

"His wife left him?" Jules asked. "When?"

"While he was in Florida. She up and moved! Packed all her clothes!"

March raised his eyebrows at Izzy and Jules. Hamish hadn't told them a thing.

"She found out about the gambling. Hamish started betting again. Double-mortgaged the house to pay off Jimmy the Knife. Plus the condo! Keiko loves that place."

"Jimmy the *Knife*?" Jules asked.

"Yeah, and they don't call him that for the way he can slice a tomato, you know what I'm saying? Loan shark. Which means you need money, he loans it. If you don't pay up, the next thing you know you're a seagull snack in a Staten Island landfill. So Keiko left him, took off to Mexico to live with her sister. I hear she's living on some beach in Mazatlán. Sweet. I mean, for her, not for Hamish. Anyway . . . if you guys are okay, I guess I should take off. I just came for these."

Joey went to one of the wooden palettes on the floor and hefted a box. "Just grabbing some stuff to sell. Kitchen stuff. Spatulas."

"Spatulas," Jules repeated.

"Yeah. Got a buddy who can sell 'em on the street for a few bucks. They're top quality. Wooden handles! Want one?"

"Oh, thanks, but, no. Don't really have a kitchen at the moment," Jules said.

Joey managed to shrug while holding a box. "Small-time stuff, I get that. But I have plans. Heather doesn't get it. Wants me to get a job. Can you believe that? I'd be the first guy in my family to get a real job. I can't let the folks down that way."

"Yeah, I hear ya," March said. "Well, great meeting you —"

"Here's the thing." Joey rested the box back on the floor. "The thing is I've got a few minor criminal infractions, right? In other words, a record. So who's going to hire me? My buddy Rico got a gig at the InvestaCorps Center. You know, where they have basketball games and concerts? Heather asks why I don't do that."

March was instantly alert. "So Rico works there?"

"He's an usher, yeah. Like I was saying, why should I go on the interview, even when I know they'll say thankyouverymuch, here's the door? Why try?"

"Maybe if you tried, you wouldn't get car keys thrown at your head," Jules said.

Joey looked puzzled.

"I mean, maybe Heather wasn't just mad about the eggs," Jules elaborated.

Joey slowly nodded. "Wow. Lightbulb! I'll have to think about that."

"So, Joey. Rico would know about security at the arena?" March asked.

"Yeah. But I can tell you it's tight. If you got any ideas —

and believe me, I had a doozy — Rico won't help. Straight as a stick. Wait. That's not what I mean; sticks can be bendy." Joey looked lost in thought.

"So . . . there's nobody you know there who could sneak us backstage?" March asked, leading him back to the point.

"Nah. I had this great idea: Rico would smuggle me in, and I'd grab the CCTV footage of the sound checks for the concerts, then start my own YouTube channel. Genius, right? Million-dollar revenue idea. Rico says no, because it would be *wrong*. I mean, that was his reason! Like I said, straight as a . . . um . . . what's the word?"

"Ruler?" Izzy asked.

"Nah, that's not it."

Joey shouldered the box. "Anyway, gotta fly. Spatulas don't wait. Hey, how about straight as a spatula! You know, if you forget the flappy part where you flip things."

"Perfect," March said.

Joey wrestled the box out the door, which slammed behind him.

"Hamish needs this more than he let on," Jules said. "It seems like everything is pushing us toward boosting that gem."

"CCTV," March said. "Izzy?"

"Yeah," Izzy said. "I'm on it."

50

THE CLIENT

The doorman looked at them dubiously, but on a word from the house phone, he pointed them toward the elevator. They zoomed upward to the seventieth floor.

They needed things. Resources. Money.

It was time to meet Ransome.

Hamish fidgeted nervously. "Okay, just don't say anything. I mean, anything much. This guy is a billionaire, but he's also just a little bit crazy."

The elevator opened into a marble vestibule with a huge bronze sculpture. A pair of double doors was straight ahead, but they were firmly shut. A voice blasted out of a hidden speaker.

"I'm in the pool. Go through the doors and up the staircase to your left."

Hamish pushed open the doors, and they walked into an apartment that arranged itself around them like a vast reception hall. Marble floors led to floor-to-ceiling windows that took in the bristling skyscrapers of Manhattan. Furniture was clustered in groups — couches, chairs, tables, shelves, enormous rugs in jewel tones. The wood was gilded, the velvet was tasseled, and the shelves groaned with crystal vases and figurines.

"This guy is almost broke?" March whispered. "This place looks like Versailles puked on itself and the Taj Mahal cleaned up."

"When the rich lose it all, they get to keep their marbles," Jules said.

One grand, twisting staircase led upward, but Hamish headed for a slightly smaller one. They climbed up to a door and pushed it open. They were in a steamy indoor pool area.

A man was swimming laps in a methodical way, his body a white distorted blur in the water. He didn't pause at the pool's edge but touched it and kept on swimming, dressed in a white cap and goggles. They stood, uncomfortably hot, on the slick wet tiles.

"Should we jump in?" Jules muttered.

It was another few minutes before the man touched the wall for the last time and stroked toward the ladder. He hoisted himself out and wrapped himself in a terry-cloth robe in a Union Jack pattern.

"This way," he said, looking like a strange alien creature with bright blue goggles and his close-fitting cap. They followed as his rubber sandals slapped on the tile.

"His toes are disgusting," Izzy whispered.

He led them to a dressing room. A long counter edged one wall, with a hair dryer and various tubes and lotions lined up next to an enormous sink. Mirrors surrounded them on three sides.

He sat at the counter and removed his cap, and damp long blondish hair fell almost to his shoulders. They watched as he carefully parted it, then swept it over his head and anchored it with bobby pins. He sprayed it with hair spray, then shot it with the dryer for a minute or so. Not until this was carefully done did he turn and look at them.

"Did you bring your kids, Hamish?" Ransome asked. "Never hear of babysitters?"

Jules bristled, but March touched his eyebrow.

Throughout his childhood with Alfie, it had been a signal. If March saw his dad on the street, but Alfie didn't want his kid to recognize him, he touched his left eyebrow. For March and Jules, it just meant *Chill and let this play out. Be ready.*

"I told you I had a special team," Hamish said. "This is Mar —"

"I don't need to know their names," he interrupted. "Your crack team is *kids?*"

"We're the kids who have two of your sapphires," Jules said.

His gaze changed from contemptuous to something else . . . something greedy and fearful. He swallowed. "Let me see them."

March reached into his pocket. He held out his palm. The stones picked up the light, and two stars suddenly flashed so brightly that they all involuntarily flinched. Were they always this blue, this sharp? Now they looked like the electric blue of a lightning storm, with an icicle star like a razor. Every time he touched them — and he tried not to touch them — they felt colder.

"Put them away!" Ransome barked.

March slowly slid them back into his pocket. He kept his eyes on Ransome. The man was beyond rattled. He was frightened.

"It's Zillah, isn't it," Izzy said. "You're afraid of her."

"Be quiet, little girl," he said. "You're too small to count."

"Why do you want them if you're so afraid of them?" Jules asked.

"Because I can control them! I'm the only one who knows how to reverse the curse." Ransome turned back to the mirror. He patted his hair. His hand was shaking. He picked up the dryer and blasted his hair for a few seconds.

Then he put down the dryer, stood, and belted his robe tighter.

"I'm leaving for London on Saturday night. I want all three stones by then. Don't give me details," he said, holding up a hand. "I know who has the last stone. Tried to buy it from her, but she won't sell. She thinks it's a lucky piece. Fool. If you can't get it from the pop star right here, you hardly stand a chance in her mansion in LA. And I can't wait while you dither. I have a pending business deal, and *I need those stones.*"

"That won't be a problem," March said.

Ransome studied March, Jules, and Izzy for a long moment. He looked at Jules longer than the others, seeming to study her face. Then he shrugged.

"London has a rich tradition of criminal urchins. I might as well take a chance on you. Snatch that necklace and run, right?"

"There's a little more involved than that," March said. "Lemon Cartelle is surrounded by security. We have to plan this. And we'll need a few things."

Ransome barked a laugh. "Listen to this kid!" he said to Hamish.

"I do listen to him," Hamish said quietly.

Ransome hesitated. "I'm not your bank, kid."

March patted his pocket. "Then we walk."

Ransome blew out a breath and shoved his hands in the pockets of his robe.

"What do you need?"

March dug in his pocket. "I've got a list. It's short."

51

GINGER TEA AND WARNINGS

March pressed the buzzer marked U. GOAWAY mounted on the brick building on West 107 Street. The three of them quickly leaned back and looked straight up. A few moments later the buzzer to release the door sounded, and March sprang forward to open it. FX had looked out the window and decided to let them in. Good start.

FX had been a makeup artist in the movie business before he realized there were more lucrative ways to use his skills. He'd known Alfie from the old days. In addition to being able to transform faces and fabricate knife wounds, gunshots, and scars, he was a clearinghouse for information on valuable property — jewels, paintings, artifacts — that were up at auction or temptingly open to steal.

They climbed the stairs to his apartment door and knocked. The door flew open.

"Hello." FX didn't smile. Maybe it was because half his neck appeared to be sawed through, and his head was half-severed.

"You're looking good," March said.

"Thanks. Ginger tea?"

"Sure."

FX ushered them inside. He started an electric kettle and left the room. Five minutes later he reappeared in tinted glasses, a brown wig, and surgical scrubs. A silk scarf was tied around his neck, and Izzy looked relieved. March had seen FX in disguise every time he met him. He still didn't know what he really looked like.

"Where's your handsome African American friend? The tall one with the eyes?"

"Staying with his mother for a while." March remembered that he'd promised himself to text Darius today.

"Aw. Mom." FX said the words without a trace of sentiment. He fussed over the tea, placing porcelain cups on an enamel tray and adding a flowered plate with small, crunchy cookies. The gang sipped and crunched politely.

"How was Paris?" FX asked. "Have a chance to hit the Louvre? I hear the *Mona Lisa* is a cinch to snatch."

"Maybe next time," March answered.

"Heard a third of the Gate of Heaven went missing."

"You don't say."

"And that foul beast Abbo in Miami lost something precious." Unexpectedly, FX beamed. "You'd make your dad proud."

The smile was gone as quickly as it appeared. FX carefully placed his cup down on the table and adjusted his glasses. "Not that it isn't a pleasure, but I'm not a people person. Can we cut to the chase? You're here for . . ."

"A little help with a disguise," March said. "I need yellow hair."

FX stared at him for a long, uncomfortable minute. "You came to me to turn you into a blond?"

"Well, it's an unusual color —" Jules started.

FX clutched his head, disturbing his wig. "And would you go to Michelangelo to create a comic book? To Julia Child for a peanut butter sandwich?"

"I think comic books are awesome," Izzy said in a small

voice. "Who knows what Michelangelo would be doing if he lived now?"

"And I bet Julia Child would make a mean peanut butter sandwich," Jules pointed out.

FX gave them a withering look. "You are reminding me that I hate children," he said.

"You could throw in a fake nose," March offered.

"Well, there you go," he said drily. "At last, a challenge."

"Plus, we'll pay."

"Now we're getting somewhere."

"Look, it's not blond. It's yellow." Jules pushed her phone toward FX.

He gave it a brief glance. "Ah. Of course. That minimally talented pop star with the Evening Star necklace."

"You know about that?"

"It is my *business* to know these things. And it's my business to know that you're getting into business you don't want to have. I admire your daring, it's true. But I don't admire your recklessness. Meaning it's over your head. Meaning you don't know who else is after it. Meaning don't come to me when it blows up in your face. There's no crying in criminality."

"The Top Cats, yeah, we know," March said. "Do you know if they're in New York?"

"No. But I'm certain that if they *are* here, they have a local contact and a place to hide. Like all good thieves, they know how to plan, and you'd hardly see them doing it. So why, foolish children, are you continuing to think it's a good idea to steal it? You're taking serious things very lightly." With one finger, FX pushed the teapot more precisely into the middle of the tray. "I would think that after your experience with the moonstones you'd have more respect."

"So you know about the curse?"

"The curse of these stones has repeated and repeated over the centuries."

FX fumbled on the bookshelf next to the table and withdrew a newspaper.

LEMON CARTELLE FIRES AGENT
Rumors Fly about Personal Struggles
Rift with Mother-Manager Trudie Cartelle
Mansion in LA Up for Sale

"Fortune and family," Izzy murmured. "Going, going, gone."

"Let me put it this way," FX said with a glance at the paper. "If you are foolish enough to go after that stone, you might be doing that young woman a favor. But you'll be passing her bad luck onto yourselves. You already have two. Three might be fatal."

"We can outrun it," March said. "As soon as we have the third, we pass it off."

"Uh-hmmm. And nothing has happened to you since you got the stones?"

"We lost all our money," Izzy blurted. "And we lost Darius!"

"It's only the beginning," FX said.

"We have a buyer," Jules said. "But we can only sell them if we have three."

"Ransome," FX said. "He's the only one who's managed to reverse the curse. Been obsessed for years. He put the word out."

"We only have two days left," March said. "And we need you to turn Jules into this." He nodded at Izzy, and she pushed her phone forward. She flicked through the images of Blue in full performance regalia.

FX looked from the images to Jules. "Of course I can do this. I'm just surprised you want to tempt fate so cruelly once again."

"You mean the moonstones? This is different."

FX shook his head slowly. "Not so different. The moonstones almost killed you and Jules. The sapphires killed your mother."

March and Jules froze.

"You know?" March asked. "You know that Alfie stole the sapphires from Ransome?"

"What are you talking about?" FX shook his head. "It was Blue."

52

PEOPLE GET BROKEN

March could feel his pounding heart. Under the table, he felt Jules's knees shaking.

"You didn't know?" FX asked. "Maggie and Beck — Blue, she calls herself now — stole the sapphires." He tapped his fingers on the tray.

Jules leaned forward, her hands clasped hard between her knees. "Tell us."

"It was their first big caper," FX said. "They got jobs as maids. The plan was for Maggie to steal the key to the study — your mother had the hands of a violinist — and hand it off to Blue. She was the lookout. Blue did the research, Maggie came up with the plan. Everything went right. Except one thing."

FX looked away.

Jules's voice was quiet. "What happened?"

"Blue changed the plan. Instead of taking off with the jewels, she gave them to Maggie without a clear plan to smuggle them out. She walked out the door, hitched a ride with the gardeners, and left Maggie there, holding the loot."

March could feel Jules holding her breath, as though it was all happening in real time. He could see it in front of him, a younger Blue making her escape, leaving her sister to take whatever punishment might rain down.

"The theft was discovered. Everyone there was searched. Maggie, too."

"She put the jewels in a vacuum-cleaner bag."

"So you know the story."

"We know Blue's version. She said that Alfie was the thief."

"Did she. Typical. Beck never liked telling the truth about anything. Thought it gave too many people an edge. She even lied to Maggie. All the time. The only person who loved her. This time Maggie felt betrayed. Stung by her own sister. When I told her about the curse, she didn't want to go through the usual channels. Not Hamish. She wouldn't even tell Alfie. They weren't married then."

"What happened?" March asked, his heart pounding the way it always did when someone mentioned his mother.

"She came to me to ask what to do. I told her that Beck knew about the curse — she'd come to me when she'd been researching the stones, so she knew about it. Maggie couldn't believe her sister would keep that kind of secret from her. Something broke for Maggie that day. Finally. They were never close again."

"Lose your fortune, lose your family," Izzy said.

"Maggie held on to the stones for years. She had no choice — they were hot. She put them in a safe-deposit box and told only me about it. After she died, I gave the key to a fence I knew. I warned him, told him the whole story, but he was willing and needed the cash. He sold them individually. Met an unfortunate accident shortly afterward."

"Lose your life," Izzy whispered.

"Did Alfie ever know any of this?" March asked.

FX shook his head. "Maybe Maggie had a little feeling left for Blue. She didn't want Alfie to have a reason to really hate her. She thought . . . maybe they'd reconcile someday. They were close as kids. Really close. You know they lost their parents, right? Brought up by an uncle who, well, wasn't a nice guy. I knew them when they first started in the business. Nobody prettier or nicer than Maggie. Charming. Making her way in the world the best she could. And Becky was the same — pretty, charming, nice as could be . . . except with Maggie it was real, it was who she was. With Beck it was an act." FX shrugged. "People get broken. Sometimes they take that and make themselves strong. Or else they don't. Those are the ones you have to be careful of. They burn you."

FX poured out the rest of the tea. "I guess that's it, the thing Maggie couldn't take anymore." He took a sip. "Becky liked the burn."

53

KARMA

SHOPPING LIST:
FIVE HUNDRED FAKE BACKSTAGE PASSES
BLUE VELVET COAT
BLUE LEOTARD
TOP HAT
YELLOW CAR

It was like he was in an ever-repeating loop and he couldn't bust out.

Blue's treachery, Alfie's fall, the family he made falling apart, a jewel to steal, a curse to break.

Karma, Hamish would have said. *You're trapped in your karma.*

Or his worst nightmare.

He picked up his phone to text Darius. What could he say?

Wasn't mad at you, dude.
I mean I was, but not for long.
I think
I think
I was just mad at my dad
Because he always blew the cash

He couldn't text that. He could barely allow the words to invade his head.

In the end, he typed one word.

Sorry
Darius didn't text back.

"I feel sick," Jules said. Her lined blue eyes looked electric. FX had gotten that azure color exactly right with contact lenses. The letters T-E-A-R ran down one cheek. It had taken them three times to get that right.

"You're sorta scary-close to Blue," Izzy said. "But it doesn't mean you *are* her."

"Look at me." March couldn't see his lemon-yellow hair, but he knew it looked bad. At least it was a wig. "I look ridiculous."

Izzy giggled. "You do. Sorry."

"Anyway, you won't even have to see Blue," March reassured Jules. "Izzy will take care of her. The routine starts with you in the rigging. It'll be dark, and Lemon will be nervous and have a spotlight in her eyes. She won't be able to tell it's not Blue, and then she's in the air twirling on the swing and lip-syncing. You know the routine?"

"I've gone over it a million times. Thanks, Izzy."

Izzy inclined her head. She'd spent the morning at a café across from the InvestaCorps Center, breaking into their CCTV feed. She'd swiped the feed of Lemon and Blue rehearsing the routine in the space. Jules had memorized it in a short amount of time.

"Standard moves," Jules said. "Lemon is a little shaky on the silks. Blue will do all the hard stuff. I mean, I will."

"You all set?" March asked Izzy. His stomach twisted when he thought of Izzy going up against Blue. Izzy had assured them that she could hack into Blue's phone with Lemon's number, which she'd gotten off March's phone during the tap transfer of the bar code. Pleading "nerves," Lemon would demand Blue meet her for one last run-through. But it had to be where no one could see her. In a room with a lock.

"Stop looking at me that way, you two," Izzy said, suddenly bristling. "Like you want to *protect* me. I'm not scared."

"We know," Jules said. "But Blue is . . ."

"Scary, yeah, I know," Izzy said. She drew herself up to her full height of not quite five feet. "I can take her."

They didn't smile. Izzy's power was awesome.

"Remember, you have to ghost your way in," March said. "Nobody can notice you."

"That's easy," Izzy said. "Nobody ever notices me."

54

SHOWTIME

The yellow Mini had been delivered that morning. Hamish nervously sat in the driver's seat. "How many times do I have to tell you? *I'm not a wheelman.*"

"Relax," March said. "You're driving us to the scene of the crime. You're not the getaway car. There's a subway station across the street."

They piled into the car, and it rattled over the cobblestones. By the time they got close to the InvestaCorps Center, the streets were crowded with young people.

"Look," Jules said. "Lots of them are carrying our tickets."

It was true. Many of the kids were clutching bright yellow tickets that they knew said KIDZPIX BACKSTAGE PASS FOR LEMON-ADES! COURTESY OF LEMON! They'd printed them up at a copy center. March knew the tickets wouldn't pass muster at the door, but they wouldn't have to. All he needed was confusion.

So many things could go wrong.

The kids wouldn't force their way in.

Izzy won't be able to hack the phone.

Jules will be stopped.

I won't be able to get close enough.

We'll be arrested.

We're back in juvie.

We never see each other again, or at least until we're thirty — or old.

We won't even recognize each other.
We will have lost everything important.
And we'll be the broken ones.

"You okay?" Jules asked him, twisting around in her seat. "Because you're muttering, and it's freaking me out."

"Fine. Hamish? Pull over here." March put his hand on the door. "I'll see you when it's over." He held out his fist. Jules and Izzy bumped it.

March got out of the car, and Hamish drove off slowly. March followed a few paces behind. Hamish drove down an alley marked NO ADMITTANCE. Crowds of kids ignored the sign, pressing their way in. A tribe of kids hammered on the stage door and then flourished their passes at the guard. They saw the car and began to chant.

"LEMON! LEMON! LEMON!"

The door to the yellow Mini swung open, and Jules strode up with Izzy. Jules walked differently, with wide strides, swaggering confidently. Like Blue. The kids fell back in disappointment.

Jules brandished her phone. It was the bar code that Lemon had sent to him, but she was moving the phone so fast that the guard couldn't scan it. Meanwhile he and his partner were trying to fend off the crowd of kids. March saw Jules wave an arm, explaining who she was.

The surge of jumping, screaming kids suddenly pushed forward and spilled through the doors. March saw one guard speaking quickly in his mouthpiece, asking for backup. Jules and Izzy were swept up in the tide and disappeared into the corridor.

Thanks to various online sources detailing celebrities backstage at concerts, awards ceremonies, and sports events, they had a pretty good idea of the layout. They had watched one particular video at least fifty times, as the cameraman followed a reporter down the hall. A freeze-frame showed one particularly out-of-the-way custodial closet with a keypad lock. Child's play for Izzy. In which, with any luck, Blue would be locked, in about — March checked his phone — twenty minutes. In the meantime that was where they would hide.

March turned and made his way through the crowd toward the front of the arena. Things were more orderly here, and he presented his bar code in the VIP line. He moved with the flow of concertgoers. He blended in with the Lemon fans and followed the signs toward the floor seats. A guy in a black T-shirt and black pants with an earphone stood, blocking the VIP floor seats. His eyes moved over the crowd.

"Rico?"

"You Joey's pal? Lemme see your ticket."

March held up his phone.

"Okay, you're up on the mezzanine, but follow me. I'll get you close to the stage."

"Awesome. I'm a complete Lemon-ade."

"She's not my thing, but enjoy."

The arena was gigantic, with a ceiling that disappeared into blackness. Rico left him in a row near the stage. "If anybody busts you, forget my name, okay?"

"You bet."

March looked above and couldn't make sense of the rigging. There were girders and beams and banks and banks of lights. Jules would have her hands full. She'd never performed in a place this big.

In minutes the lights dimmed, and the show began. March counted off the acts, who strutted their stuff with deafening bass. Roars greeted every award winner. Soon the front of the stage was a writhing, jumping mass of fans. It looked good for the cameras, so the ushers didn't interfere.

The minutes ticked by. March felt his phone buzz in his pocket. It was Izzy.

All clear.

That meant she was standing outside the closet, Blue locked inside. Everyone else stared at the BooBoo Girls onstage, but March looked up. He saw a slender figure climbing the rigging. For a moment he was afraid it was Blue. Then he recognized his twin as she balanced high above the crowd and reached for her silks.

Showtime.

55

WHEN THE STARS ARE NOVAS

The lights dimmed. The crowd screamed. Lemon Cartelle walked out onto the stage. She didn't acknowledge the screams and applause, just stood and waited for the noise to die down slightly. Then the music began and she sang the famous first lines to the theme song to the biggest movie of the year, *Dissolution*.

"When the stars are novas,
When the tides run out to the sea,
It will be you and me.
Our day will come
When all is broken in pieces,
And a cloud covers the sun we'll run . . ."

The silks dropped from the rigging above. Was March the only person to notice that her hand was shaking as she grabbed them? March squinted. He could just make out Jules, standing on a small platform above, ready for her cue. She would do most of the acrobatics. Lemon would primarily swing and sing.

As always, he marveled at Jules's nerve, so high above the stage that he could only see the glint of her costume.

Lemon's voice slithered out over the audience now as she was slowly lifted into the air. The crowd went crazy. March began to snake his way closer.

"And the crash and the burn,
And the fire and the ice.
Just bring us to paradise . . ."

Jules swung down, circling Lemon. Her knees wrapped in the fabric, swinging, making Lemon look better by taking all the real risks.

Jules had gone over the moves in her head, rehearsing on the floor, earbuds in. He'd seen her, eyes closed, learning the routine by heart. He could see now that it helped that Lemon was nervous. Jules had to help her, twirling the silks to get her moving.

He felt his phone buzz in his pocket and took it out.

SOS she's out

Her GPS on phone shows movement

Must be a vent in there she got out

Searching but

She's not anywhere

I'm standing right by the stage. I see the moving dot. I DON'T SEE HER!!!!!

March swallowed and keyed in a command.

Look up

After a moment Izzy's reply buzzed in.

Up in the scaffolding. She's heading for the silks!

56

MIDAIR BATTLE

March craned his neck, chilled at the sight of Blue making her way fearlessly along the metal scaffolding above.

Desperately, he moved his gaze to Jules. She hadn't seen Blue. He couldn't warn her. He watched, helpless, as she twisted upside down, wrapping her ankles in the fabric and letting go, twirling fast, faster.

Blue reached the silks and grabbed the one Jules was on. The movement threw Jules off balance, and she knocked into Lemon. The crowd gasped, March right along with them. Lemon's voice went on singing — now it was clear she was lip-syncing — but her mouth made an O of surprise.

Jules looked up then and saw Blue. She barely hesitated. If March didn't know better, he would think that this was part of the choreography, how she managed to wrap one knee around Lemon's silk to steady herself.

Blue yanked the silk, giving it a hard twirl, and Jules jerked to the left but was able to turn it into an acrobatic move, swinging upside down from one of the free silks, while Lemon continued to sing. Caught between her own silks and Lemon's, Jules began a series of moves to get clear, climbing Lemon's silk with one hand.

Blue slithered down the silks, one arm raised in triumph, still holding Jules's in the other, and the crowd cheered. March's heart was in his throat. Every second was agony.

He could see that Jules was off balance. He couldn't help his twin.

He could only watch.

Wait for her to fall.

Like Alfie.

He couldn't move. The oily black river moved through him and filled his lungs, and he couldn't breathe. *Zillah.*

Blue was close to Jules now, her face a grimacing mask. While they twirled and flipped one hundred feet above the stage, they grabbed each other's silks, trying to upend each other. It was a desperate fight. The crowd roared, thinking it was all part of the show, part of a song about battles and destruction, and Lemon kept on singing.

Jules swung out, gaining control of her silks, and began to flip in a series of moves to bring her closer to Lemon, hanging from her armpits, then her knees, then her ankles. Suddenly Blue swung after her and hooked an ankle around the fabric. She yanked it hard, and Jules began to slide, falling toward the stage below. The crowd screamed. March felt his lungs constrict. *Jules!*

At the last moment Jules grabbed a silk and hung on, bouncing. March saw her muscles shaking. He could see panic on her face but doubted anyone else could tell. As Blue began to swing, preparing to launch at her, Jules gave a midair dive so breathtakingly crazy the crowd erupted in a great roar.

As the closing notes of the song began, Jules bounced by her ankles. Then in one smooth move she grabbed Lemon's silks and slid down right above Lemon's head, letting her belt out the last notes.

March knew the spotlight would leave Lemon's face for

just a moment, as yellow light traveled from her ankles to her head as she spun upside down. Blue had designed the routine to cover Lemon's inexperience and also show herself off.

"When cold oceans boil
When heaven falls . . ."

March tensed in agony. Jules had managed to slide down the silk, one arm lifted.

". . . I will hear your caaaaalllll."

The lights went out, then flashed on, and Lemon flipped to hang by her ankles, twirling while the audience went crazy. . . .

March squinted, but he could no longer see Jules and Blue, just shapes. Then he caught the flash of someone flipping over and over, straight down toward the stage. The two somersaulted to the ground. Lemon wobbled. The other figure hit the stage perfectly.

Jules.

The relief made him cry out loud. He could breathe again. His yell was lost in the crowd's applause. Lemon lifted her arms, launched herself at the crowd gathered around the stage, and crowd-surfed. As Blue slid down to the stage, Jules launched herself after Lemon. March had squeezed himself to the front, waiting.

Lemon and Jules crowd-surfed toward the aisle. Lemon gave Jules one aggrieved backward look for following her. That wasn't in the script.

March was close, closer now, holding Lemon up and cheering as he moved forward toward Jules, who was being carried aloft by the crowd. His hand slipped into Jules's pocket. If Jules had managed to do it, it would be a miracle.

But she was a miracle worker.

He ripped apart the Velcro, and his fingers found the necklace. He slipped it out smoothly and quickly, a classic pickpocket pull.

And then he was gone, melted back into the crowd before Jules had regained her feet, racing toward the exit as a triumphant Lemon acknowledged the cheers and Blue's sharp gaze raked the crowd.

57

THE ROAD TO PRISON

As he made his way to the exit, March dunked the yellow wig in a trash can and pulled on a baseball cap. He bought a bag of popcorn and munched while he walked, trying to look casual even though his heart was about to bust through his ribs. Izzy should already be outside. Jules should be in the restroom, taking off the makeup and costume. Blue could be anywhere.

He passed fans buying T-shirts and pushed open the front doors, taking a gulp of warm September air that felt full of rain.

Izzy melted out of the background and stood by his side. "Did she get it?"

"Yeah. But we have to get out of here, fast."

Jules rounded the corner, heading toward them, her hair now in her customary spiky style, wearing jeans and sneakers that Izzy had secreted in the bathroom for her.

"Subway," March said, and they dashed across the street toward the entrance.

They started down the stairs. Coming toward them, emerging out of the darkness, was Blue.

"Going somewhere?" she asked.

March had known that the subway connected to an entrance within the arena. He hadn't expected Blue to ambush them, though.

He vowed it would be his last mistake.

"Problem?" he asked.

"Yeah. I'd say so. First tiny missy there locks me in a closet. Then Jules takes over my silks."

"Guess I just missed the spotlight," Jules said.

"And Lemon's necklace is missing," Blue said. "There's that. Are you insane? Do you know how many cameras are in that arena? Not just security, but TV? Phones? I'm guessing it will take about ten minutes for you to be all over the Internet. And then you're on the road to prison."

"Maybe," Jules said. "But maybe they'll think it's you."

"You little . . ." Blue slowly mounted the stairs.

March waited for her to get to the top. There was no reason to run. Not yet. In the meantime he looked without seeming to look, the way Alfie had taught him. People heading for the subway, coming up the stairs, parting around them. A hot dog vendor to his right. Someone handing out flyers on his left. Traffic moving. Stopping. Taxi being hailed. Black SUV with tinted windows, the kind that celebrities use, changing lanes, probably dropping someone at the concert, or picking someone up.

"So before I alert the police, let's make a deal," Blue said as she reached them. "I can make all this go away."

"The police? That's the last thing you'd do!" Jules scoffed.

"I'm leading the straight life now," Blue said. "I'm a pop star, remember?"

"A legend in your own mind," March said.

"Just got off my ten-city European tour," Blue said. "Sold-out venues."

"You had to cancel the last three cities because of low ticket sales," Jules said. "Only four people showed up in Copenhagen."

"Lemon Cartelle is my best friend," Blue continued. "Who do you think they're going to believe — me or some kids?"

"I wish people would stop saying that," Izzy said. "Even if it's true."

"I'll bring her back the necklace. You can just take off. We're family. I owe you."

"We're not giving you anything," Jules said.

March tensed. *Black SUV blocking crosswalk.*

And then suddenly a word from out of nowhere floated into his head. *Copenhagen.*

Jules had said *Copenhagen.* And earlier, when she'd been reciting the cities of Blue's tour: Dubrovnik.

Another black SUV making a turn, blocking the corner.

Her tour schedule.

Copenhagen.

What had Dukey said?

. . . jobs in Milan, Dubrovnik, Copenhagen . . .

. . . skills your sister has . . .

"You're after the sapphire, too," March said. "You're a Top Cat!"

Blue smiled.

58

THE CHASE

"Five o'clock," March said. "I'll turn them over at five o'clock."

It was a code he'd devised to alert the gang to danger. It basically meant *This is a red alert, follow me.* And if he was the twelve o'clock position, their escape would be at five.

Blue scowled. "What are you —"

But she said the rest to empty air. They were gone.

March charged straight at the black SUV, Jules and Izzy right behind him. He just caught a glimpse of the startled driver as he leapfrogged up onto the hood, scrambled over the windshield to the roof, and then slid down, hitting the street. Jules and Izzy were on his heels.

They had surprise on their side, but March knew that it bought them less than a minute. They flew across the side street. March chanced a look back. A furious Blue was already screaming at the driver and getting in the car. That was the one that worried him. The one that was pointing in the right direction.

The map is not the territory.

Thanks to Alfie, March had done his homework. He already knew Brooklyn, but he made sure he knew it better over the past few days, studying street maps online, pacing out the neighborhood around the arena while Izzy pulled off the hack. He knew the location of every subway stop, every alley.

His best bet would be to head toward Prospect Park. It

would be crowded with families and joggers and people strolling in the warm September air. Plenty of opportunities to blend in.

He thought all this at lightning speed while cutting down an alley, Jules and Izzy at his side.

"Two blocks to the park," he told the others as they ran. "We can lose them there."

They started across the street, but the SUV suddenly roared down the street, going against traffic. Horns blared, but the car kept moving, the driver expertly twisting through the vehicles trying to get out of the way. Heading right for them.

"Other way!" March shouted, and they reversed direction.

Only to face the other SUV barreling toward them. It grazed a van as it surged forward.

"Subway," March panted. "Three blocks."

They dived right, down a crowded shopping street. Weaving through the pedestrians, they dodged strollers and dog leashes and couples holding hands. They reached the subway, but yellow police tape was over the entrance and a SUSPENDED SERVICE sign was attached to it. March hit the railing in frustration.

"Another one in five blocks," he panted.

They made a sharp left, then a right. The SUV was ahead. March reversed and made a left. Every time they saw the car, they reversed and dived down a different street. Their leg muscles were burning now. They were close to worn out.

And then they were lost.

The thing about Brooklyn is, March thought, *you can go a block or two and be in a completely different neighborhood.*

Suddenly the street was run-down, deserted. Some of the buildings looked abandoned, leaning into one another like wobbly bowling pins about to fall. But this was Brooklyn, where real estate was king, and in the middle of the block a twelve-story brick building that still had a faded HOTEL painted on the front sported a sagging banner reading LUXURY CONDOS FOR SALE NOW. The front was boarded up, but he could see the long neck of a crane.

A dark SUV appeared at the end of the street. It stopped, blocking the end of the street.

Behind them, another SUV appeared, blocking that exit as well.

59

WE ARE NOBODY
WE ARE NOWHERE

"When in doubt, go up," Jules said. "That's my motto. Look at the roof. One after the other, super close."

"I wouldn't call it *super* close," March said.

"I'll tell you something I know for sure — those guys won't jump."

"What about Blue?"

Jules set her jaw. "We can handle Blue."

A man whose muscles bulged out of his close-fitting jacket emerged from the car.

"I have an idea. Let's go up," March said.

Jules scaled the wooden construction wall in two seconds flat, then reached down for Izzy. March boosted himself up and over.

They stood in a dirt pit, surrounded by heavy moving equipment. Two Dumpsters were full of junk — couches, armchairs, sinks, carpeting. Jules shaded her eyes as she scanned the building. A heavy fabric tube ran down one side of the building, a way for the workers to throw trash out. It ended in another Dumpster.

"They're taking it apart from the inside," Jules said. "But it doesn't look like they've gotten far. Hopefully there will still be floors."

"Yeah," March said. "That's key."

"Don't look so nervous," she said. "We used to set up pitches in abandoned buildings all the time."

"Sure," Izzy murmured as they pushed aside a tarp to enter. "I'm sure they're just kidding with that 'Danger No Admittance' sign."

Inside were the remains of a tiled floor, partially jack-hammered away. Pale murals ghosted the walls. Part of the ceiling was gone. The musty smell of sadness rose in their nostrils, and they stopped short.

"This is the creepiest place I've ever seen," Izzy whispered.

"C'mon," Jules said, heading for the stairs.

It was impossible to tell what color the carpet had been — green? Tan? Now it was the color of sludge, with a thick coat of dirt. Footprints from construction shoes merged and separated, creating a pattern of industry and grime. They reached the first floor. The doors had been taken off the rooms and were stacked at one end of the hallway. As they rounded the landing, heading for the next flight of stairs, they passed the open rooms. Quick glimpses of broken dressers, an ancient TV, a busted phone, broken tile in a gaping doorway that led to a cracked toilet. A teddy bear was propped up against one wall, wearing a pair of underwear on its head. On the wall of one room someone had written IF YOU WANT A TRUE FRIEND TRY A RAT and WE ARE NOBODY WE ARE NOWHERE.

"Squatters," March said. "People lived here."

Jules grimaced. "Yeah, Joey's garage is looking good."

They climbed the second staircase. From below they heard a noise. Someone smashing into something and cursing.

The gang was here. Footsteps rang out against the tiled floor.

March felt the sapphires, heavy in his pocket. Just like Alfie, he always kept the loot on him. *Safer that way*, Alfie used to say. *Never trust a landlord.*

Should he throw them down into the lobby? Would the men go away? These were guys with weapons. Serious stuff.

Jules read his mind. "We still have a chance. Let's just get to the roof."

They raced up the stairs and burst out onto the roof. The sky was lowering, and a few drops of rain fell. Jules whipped her head around, studying her options.

"It's farther than it looks," she said. She glanced at Izzy. March knew what she was thinking. They might make it, but Izzy was too small to jump that distance.

"I can do it," Izzy said.

Jules slowly shook her head.

"Then I'll stay," Izzy said. "You go. They won't do anything to me."

"I'm not leaving you here with those guys, are you nuts?" March said.

"Nobody's leaving anybody," Jules said. She pointed to a pile of lumber. "We can use one like a plank. Come on."

March hoisted the plank of wood. Izzy and Jules took an end, and March steadied the center. With Jules directing, they lifted it up, and then released it. It smashed down on the adjoining roof.

March looked over the side and gulped. With that double-height lobby, fifteen stories down.

"You know the first rule," Jules said.

"Don't look down."

Izzy swallowed. "What's the second?"

"Don't fall off," March said.

Jules dusted her hands on her pants. "It's about fifteen seconds of keeping your balance, and then you're done. We get rid of the plank, and we're out of here. They'll think we're hiding down there. By the time they stop searching, we'll be gone."

He nodded, feeling the blood rushing in his ears.

"I'll go first," Jules said. "Then, Iz, you stay behind me. It can hold both of us. Hang on to my shirt if you have to."

"But that will throw you off balance."

"It won't."

Jules balanced on the narrow plank and started across. Izzy took a deep, steadying breath. Jules looked back.

"I'm okay," Izzy said. "I can do it."

Jules walked across, never looking down, one foot hitting directly in front of the other. Izzy seemed to drift across like a dandelion seed. They stepped off onto the roof on the other side, and March discovered he'd been holding his breath. He exhaled.

March looked across the expanse at Jules. He took a few steps on the board, keeping his eyes on his sister. He could do this if he didn't think about Alfie. He shuffled forward, keeping his eyes on his destination as Jules had taught him.

Don't think about that moment Alfie had teetered on the edge, had almost saved himself. Don't think about how he fell, his body turning.

Halfway across he heard the slam of the rooftop door. He stopped, his arms windmilling as a burst of adrenaline shot up from his tingling toes.

"Keep it steady," Jules called. "Just keep going."

"How many are behind me?"

"Just keep going," Jules repeated. "You can move, uh, a little faster, though." He heard someone running across the roof. His foot slipped, and he hit the plank hard on one knee, gripping the edge and just saving himself from plummeting to the ground below. His ears rang with Izzy's scream.

Dizzy and barely holding on, March focused on the brick wall of the building. He could barely make out the ghost lettering on the wall.

HOTEL AMSTERDAM

Amsterdam. Where Alfie had died, falling, smashing against the hard stones.

He was back there again, after a year of grief, a year of making a family, and he hadn't really gotten anywhere. He was just like his old man, falling and dying, not for something noble, not for his country or justice or right, but because of a handful of gems.

"March!" Jules's call was so sure. "YOU CAN DO THIS."

Izzy's voice was louder than he'd ever heard it. "MOVE!"

Fifteen stories up is no time to philosophize, kid.

March slowly began to rise.

"NO!" Jules screamed, and the plank lurched to the side. He gripped it hard as sweat poured into his eyes. Jules held on to the plank on her side, and Izzy threw herself on the end of it, trying to weigh it down.

"Don't bother," Blue called. "These guys are strong."

The plank bumped up, then down.

"Just reverse-crawl back, March," Blue said. "All I want are the stones. But I'll get them off the pavement down there if I have to."

March looked at Jules with despair. Lost in a long moment in which everything mattered. They would lose to Blue again.

Then the plank was yanked backward, out of Jules's hands. March went down to keep his balance, cheek against the wood, straddling it. He risked a look over his shoulder. The two burly guys were pulling the plank back onto the roof, straight toward Blue.

60

SHOWDOWN

Inch by inch the plank moved, scraping against the roof edge. March could only hang on.

He was cooked.

He could see the desperate looks on the faces of his friends. Suddenly Jules turned and ran across the roof. At the same time the plank gave one last heave. Someone grabbed him hard and threw him on the roof. Gravel bit his cheek, and he tasted blood in his mouth.

There were four of them. Plus Blue. The men looked far from friendly. Three of them were dressed in suits that didn't hide their muscles, their strength, or a telltale bulge near the hip that Alfie had told him to always, always beware of. *You see that, you just reverse and go out the door. No matter what the prize.* But somehow it was the shorter one, the slim one, who scared him the most. Something about the eyes. March remembered a man on a street in Paris, turning, seeing him, and how that hatred had flared, all the way across the distance separating them.

It was the wheelman in the Paris heist. The captain on the boat.

He smiled and crouched down next to March. He made his fingers into a gun and poked March in the temple. "Bang."

Terror shuddered through him. He couldn't feel his legs.

"I can only hold them back so long, March," Blue said.

March reached into his pocket. He handed over Lemon's necklace.

"Keep going," Blue said. "You're your father's son. I know you keep the loot."

He had run out of time. He fished out the Evening Star and held it up. But before Blue could take it, it was snatched out of his hand by the slender man.

Blue rose to her feet in an instant. "Wait a second, Zef! This is *my deal*, remember? I handle the stones!"

"Shut up," the man said. "What shall we do with your nephew when this is done, Blue? Throw him off the roof?"

"Why bother?" Blue said. "He's harmless now."

"He's seen my face."

"All right, then," Blue snapped. "It's up to you. Whatever you do to people who get in your way."

"And you feel that *you* are not in the way?" Zef smiled. "Without Dmitri here to protect you? He fell under your spell. Not me."

Blue faltered for an instant. The fear that flickered on her face passed so quickly it was converted into a shake of her hair. "That sounds like a threat."

March staggered to his feet. He took a half step back.

"What, you will tell Dmitri? He's my brother. He listens to me. You're just . . ." The man waved a hand. "A detail."

"A detail that got you here," Blue said. "A detail that got you a safe house. You're the one who blew the deal in Miami!"

"And you blew this one! Locked in a closet by a little girl!"

March watched as Blue visibly contained her temper. She did what she always did when cornered, reverse direction and try a different way. Her voice was level. "Listen, this kid isn't stupid. That could be a fake. March, give me the other one."

March waited. The heat of the argument was too intense for the two of them to stop.

"Do you think I'm a fool? Is that it? You play with me? You think I've clawed my way to where I am because I'm a fool?" Zef's face was dark with anger. The bodyguards stood, their faces rigid, but their gazes flicking from Blue to Zef.

Which was good, because nobody was looking at March. He took another step back. March's legs shook. He didn't think he was capable of running away. But the tension between Blue and Zef was giving him something, the tiniest of moments to just *do something*. But what?

Behind Blue he saw a tiny flare of movement. A hand curling over the roof's edge. Then Jules's head popped up cautiously. How did she do it? Even Jules couldn't climb air. He gave the slightest shake of his head. Any moment they could turn and see her. With a tilt of her head, she told him to come to her. Somehow. Now.

It was his last chance, and he knew it.

March picked up fistfuls of gravel, threw them straight at the faces of the bodyguards, and hurtled toward his twin.

61

DUMPSTER DIVING

Jules yanked him forward into thin air.

He felt himself plummeting. Terror made him lose his breath. He couldn't even scream.

Then the silks stretched to their maximum and held. Jules was gritting her teeth, holding him while they bounced, once, twice, in the seat she'd made of fabric. It was strong enough to hold them both.

March's gaze raked the building. He could only guess that his twin had climbed *up* the exterior trash chute, then somehow managed to jump onto the half-demolished fire escape. The silks were anchored to a hook near the roofline.

She began to swing, hard and fast. "Brace yourself," she panted. "We're going down that thing."

"What?" March asked, just as the next swing landed him in the gigantic plastic chute.

March's legs shot out, almost as though her command had gone straight to his muscles. He wasn't thinking now; he was only moving, bracing himself against the tough material of the chute. Jules's face was white with strain, and she unwrapped herself from the silks.

"We're going to have to crab-walk down," she said.

"All the way?"

"I got up this way. We can get down this way. GO!"

Choking on dust and grime and grit and whatever

residue still remained in the chute, his throat and nostrils clogged with mildew and debris, March half fell, half crab-walked down. He fell the last few feet, straight into the Dumpster. Out of breath, choking, he lay there for an instant before Jules landed next to him and Izzy's face popped over the side.

"Are you okay?"

Up on the roof, he saw the heads looking down. Even from here he could feel the blind rage of Zef and Blue.

"Yeah. They're going to come after us," Jules said. She waved at Blue, a final taunt. How she had the nerve he didn't know.

March pulled himself up and over the edge of the Dumpster. Izzy steadied him as he landed. Jules leaped out like a gazelle.

"Time to go," March said.

They didn't stop running until they got to the subway. They changed lines three times, then circled back at last to Joey's garage. When they got inside, Hamish was sitting in the office, slumped over the desk. The gang hardly recognized him. He had the shoulders of a ruined man.

He stood up when he saw them and closed his eyes. "When you didn't show up . . . I thought . . ." He stopped, letting out a long breath. When he opened his eyes again, they saw his relief. "I'm glad you're back."

"Something did happen. The Top Cats showed up," Jules said. "And Blue. But we're all okay."

"They got the necklace. And the Evening Star." March

held out the remaining sapphire. "But we still have the Morning Star. They got distracted."

"Maybe this will be enough for Jimmy the Knife," Izzy said. At Hamish's look of surprise, she said, "Joey told us everything."

"Ah," Hamish said. "I don't know why I trust that kid."

"We'll give you our cut," March said, with a quick glance at the others. They nodded.

"Still not enough," Hamish said with a twisted smile. "And I wouldn't do it anyway. I never go back on a deal." He walked toward them slowly. "It's time for me to say good-bye. I'm going to take a ride on the Pokey Express."

"You're going to jail?" Izzy exclaimed.

"No, I'm taking a ride on the Pokey Express," Hamish said, showing them a bus ticket from a company called Pokey Express. "It's a slow route to Saratoga, but it gets you there for fifteen bucks. I'm going to throw the rest of what I've got at one of the horses, see if I can get out of this mess, then crawl on my knees to Mexico and ask Keiko to take me back."

"You can't do that," Jules said. "You said you'd never gamble again."

"Plus, um, it doesn't work," Izzy said. "Remember?"

"I'm out of options, young yogis," Hamish said. "It's this or a long ride on a short pier with Jimmy the Knife, and then I wash up in New Jersey."

March gripped the stone. What was it all for, then? He'd almost been killed for this cursed stone. He'd had all three, and he'd lost two. Lost his fortune.

Just like his old man.

Izzy brightened. "It's a text from Darius!" She looked

down at her phone. She gasped, her hand flying to her mouth. "No!"

She handed the phone to March.

The text read:

TOP CATS GOT ME
THEY WANT THE STONE

62

KIDNAPPED

March felt something drop, a weight that went down, down, threatening to drag him with it. Like drowning in a black river, tied to a bagful of rocks.

Inside he was screaming.

Not Darius.

No.

He handed the phone to Jules. She read it while Hamish looked over her shoulder.

"How . . ." Jules said. "He's in Florida with Mikki."

"Text him back, Iz," March said, shaking.

What do u mean?

The next text came quickly.

That will be your last communication with your friend until we have the stone.

March took out his own phone with fingers that trembled. He dialed Mikki's number. He swallowed against the dryness in his throat. Fear had wrapped itself around him, strangling him.

"Hello, sugar," Mikki answered. "You missing the sunshine?"

She didn't know. He couldn't speak.

"March?"

"When was the last time you saw Darius?"

"Last night. At dinner. I made us tuna fish salad. Isn't it funny how you say tuna fish, but you don't say that for any other fish? Like, you don't say swordfish fish. Or salmon fish. It's just dumb, isn't it? I'm not going to say it anymore. I'm just going to say tuna. Anyway, I didn't see him this morning because he left to go fishing with Dimmy."

"You mean he's still not there?"

"Well, he might be. I just got home myself. I'll look in his room. You hang on."

March heard her footsteps down the hall. The creak of a door.

"That's funny. He's not here. And he's not by the pool. They said they'd be back by lunchtime. Then Dimmy texted me, told me they were having such a good time, they were staying out until dinner."

"Dimmy."

"I was happy Dimmy asked him fishing, because you know what? They weren't getting along so good. He didn't want to go, I could tell, but I kicked him under the table. He went to make his mama happy, because that's the kind of boy he is . . . March?" Mikki's voice wavered. "You're starting to worry me, just a little bit. And you know I don't like to worry."

Dimmy.

Dmitri.

Dimmy.

Harmless, friendly Dimmy with the Euro accent and the beat-up truck, who had showed up out of nowhere. Dimmy, who'd always been around, clipping hedges or planting flowers by the pool *where they'd planned the second heist.* Wearing headphones so they thought he couldn't hear them.

Dimmy was Dmitri. Dimmy was the boss.

Waiting for them to steal the sapphire so his crew could steal it from them.

"March?"

The hardest thing to do is to say the thing there are no words for. The thing he should have said to her son.

"I'm sorry," March whispered.

63

WHERE THE FAULT LIES

When March finally hung up with Mikki, his legs shook so badly he felt as though he'd run ten hard miles.

Izzy sat in a corner, her face against her knees. Jules sat on one side of her. Hamish sat on the damp floor, his head in his hands.

March crossed to Izzy and sat on the other side. He exchanged a glance with Jules. It felt like Zillah was there in the room with them, whispering in their ears. *Failure. Loss. Pain.*

"We're cursed," Izzy said, her mouth against her knee. "Zillah's not done with us."

It isn't the curse, March thought in despair. *It's me.* If it hadn't been for him, Darius would be here. He'd left him with Dimmy.

His fault. Shame filled him, bitter and bleak.

"What did Mikki say?" Jules asked.

"She's going to Dimmy's house," March said. "I don't think they're still in Florida. They're bringing Darius here. He'd have to be at the transfer, when we give them the sapphire."

He took Izzy's phone and typed back.

We'll give you the sapphire.

The reply buzzed through.

We'll text details.

Hamish's face was sagging with worry. "Do you have an idea?" he asked. "A plan?"

March stared at him for a second. There were still times, even now, when he looked to the adult in the room and thought, *Tell me what to do.* But the adult was looking at him.

"We give them the sapphire," he said. "There's no plan except that. We can't gamble with Darius's life."

"I agree," Hamish said. "But if they double-cross us . . ."

March remembered Zef on the roof. *He's seen my face.* Dukey in Paris. *If you can ID them, you're dead.* The words bounced against cement. Boomeranged around March's skull. Hard. Painful.

His fault.

64

DESPERATE THINKING

March woke with a start. He was instantly awake. Instantly afraid.

He heard Jules and Izzy breathing sleep-breaths, gently burrowed in their beanbags. He was glad they had finally dropped off to sleep. Exhaustion had swept over them. Tomorrow would be a hard, hard day.

He flipped over on his back and stared at the ceiling.

The words he never said. The words he *did* say. The look he gave. The gesture he didn't make, the text he didn't send.

Darius had stayed in Florida because of him.

His fault.

For thinking that a house was so important, that it was the only way to get his life back. Sure, it was Alfie's dream. But was it his?

That place was just walls and floors.

He thought back on that day, at their shock that everything could just be gone. Sitting on the floor, he'd made a promise that he'd get it all back. Without even thinking about *what* he needed to get back.

March pressed his fingers against his eyes. He was so tired. He needed sleep. But he needed to think this through. He was missing something.

Where was Darius? That was the question.

What was the thread he needed to pull?

He thought of Blue's secretive smile at every encounter they'd had with her. At the gym, at the subway, on the roof.

No wonder she was so smug. She had the Top Cats for backup. Dukey had said they had a contact in the United States. Blue had been that contact. She'd been working with them all along.

Blue had been the thief in the Paris apartment. The one walking away, up the hill in Paris. Just like she'd walked away that foggy night in Amsterdam.

He'd been so stupid not to see it.

Stupid. A word Darius would never throw at him. No matter what.

Blue was a monster. Taunting them. Taunting Jules.

Still playing the poor little girl? Even in your fancy town house with the pool?

March bolted up.

The pool.

Blue knew Alfie's apartment. She'd been there. But she hadn't been there since they'd bought the building. Since they'd put in that stupid lap pool they hardly ever used.

The safe house. Blue had said she'd found them a safe house. That's where they'd stash Darius.

And he knew right where he'd be.

Home.

65

BREAKING AND ENTERING

March stole through the streets like mist. He knew how to hide from the moonlight. He made his way down the dark streets, hoping with every passing block that he was right.

Right to come alone. He would scope out the building. If he was wrong, he'd be back in Brooklyn before dawn.

If he was right . . . well, he'd make that decision when he came to it.

He turned the corner of his block and slid from shadow to shadow. Stood across the street, away from the streetlamp.

Nothing. Not a flicker of light or movement. The gates to the alley were closed. He waited another moment, then sprinted across the street and clambered over the gate. At the top he looked down and saw a black SUV. Tinted windows and the same license plate as the one that had chased them. His heart hammering, he dropped over to the other side.

He was right. Rage made his brain a swarm of angry bees. He took deep breaths, steadying himself. What to do. What to do. Text Izzy and Jules?

Put them in danger the way he'd done with Darius?

Afraid to leave, afraid to go. It was so close to dawn. Anything could happen tomorrow. He only had now.

If Darius was here he needed to know. It was *past* need;

it was hunger and anger and compulsion. His friend, his brother, could be in there. He couldn't walk away.

Carefully he balanced on the trash can. He moved the metal shim, placed the key in the lock. He pushed open the window. Waited, listening. Trying to hear over the thundering of his heart.

He slipped inside and landed noiselessly. He started for the service stairs. They would bring him to the back corridor of the bedroom floor, or upstairs into the kitchen. March thought fast. The bedroom level first.

He climbed quickly. When he got to the bedroom level, he eased open the door. The corridor was dark. He moved soundlessly past a storage room, past the bedrooms, to peer around the wall to the common area.

The Top Cats had furnished the room with a few pieces. A table crowded with empty cans and takeout containers, a sofa, a couple of folding chairs. Not much.

Snoring.

A dark shape on the couch. An outflung arm. One of the goons from the roof.

March let out a shaky breath. Where was Darius? There were at least four goons in the house. Probably Dimmy — Dmitri — was here, too. They would take the best rooms. And they would shove Darius anywhere.

March's brain lit up. The storage room. The small room near the stairs that Jules had told them was planned as a maid's room. They'd laughed about that. Imagine having a maid! It wasn't long before they *wished* they had a maid. They had always meant to make a chore list. Never had.

They'd crammed their sports equipment and old computer parts and broken stuff in there. March tried the door.

It was locked, a good sign. He leaned over with his lockpicking equipment.

Quietly, he spun the pick, listening, feeling for the tumbler. Open.

He pushed open the door an inch, then another.

Darius lay on the floor.

66

BROTHERS

His heart stopped. Then Darius settled himself in his sleep. He was alive.

March wanted to fall to his knees and sob like a kid.

One wrist was handcuffed to the pipe that ran a few inches above the floor. But Darius was here. Darius was alive.

He put a hand on Darius's shoulder and another over his mouth. Darius's eyes widened when he saw March.

"Dude, I'm so glad to see you," March whispered.

"I think I've got you beat."

March clasped his shoulder and squeezed. He bent over with his pick as Darius held up his wrist.

"Dimmy got me," Darius said. "I knew the guy was bad news, but I had no clue . . . He's a Top Cat! The boss!"

"I know. And Blue is with the gang."

"I know," Darius said. "I heard her talking to Dimmy."

"Is she here?"

"Nah, she's still stringing along her pop star, blaming the heist on you — good going, by the way. Hey, how's my girl Izzy?"

"I'd fill you in on everything, but can it wait? We have less than an hour until dawn. They could wake up anytime."

Darius reached for his shoes and shoved his feet into them. He started to tie his laces. "Ransome is the buyer. I don't know where, but a deal is going down. They got two sapphires."

"Yeah. We have the other one. Trading it for you."

"Appreciate it."

"You're almost worth it."

They started toward the door, but Darius stopped.

"They're not going to give up, you know," he said. "I've spent a day and a night with these guys, and I want to tell you, they are serious."

March remembered his terror on the roof. "Yeah."

"We double-cross them now, they'll come after us. And the fact that we're kids? Doesn't make any diff."

"I got that."

"We've always meant nothing," Darius said. "I learned that quick from being in the system. Never got a decent foster situation going. When I complained about stuff, I was shut down. Didn't have a voice. Look at Izzy. It took her years to say *anything*, and she's just about the smartest human on the planet."

March shifted restlessly. "D, we've really gotta *move*."

"I'm just saying, we cross them now, we won't be able to run fast enough or far enough. And we'll be back where we started."

"Then we start out with nothing all over again. We did okay."

"Got a question. How are you getting me out? I don't fit through that window."

"I figured we'd go out the front door."

"There are guards on the exits. And they won't be sleeping."

"Then we give them the Morning Star and walk out."

"That isn't going to work, Marco. These guys are bad dudes. The worst. We'll never make it through that door.

I've seen all their faces, heard their names. The stone is all the leverage we got."

"Then we make a run for it."

"We'll never make it and you know it. "Darius shook his head. "Plus Mikki can ID Dmitri. Knows stuff about him. He found her going through his computer. I'm guessing she was looking for girlfriends, a wife. Doesn't matter. He doesn't know if she knows something that could bring him down, something that she'll only put together now that she knows who he is. He told me to scare me." Darius's gaze was hunted. "It did."

March leaned against the wall and closed his eyes. Fear had drained him of everything. "I don't know anything anymore. What should we do?"

Darius smiled his slow, easy smile. "You know what? That's the first time you ever asked me that. You're the one with the ideas, Professor."

"Well, I'm all out," March said. "I don't think we can beat this."

"That's not like you."

"I don't know what I am," March admitted. "I'm not my dad, that's for sure. Because the only thing I'm caring about right now is family." March struggled to get the words out. "I'm sorry about . . . everything. I wasn't fair. I make mistakes all the time. I'm sorry I called you stupid. You're *annoying*, but you're not stupid."

"I'm sorry I fell for the sting," Darius said. "I should have seen it a mile off." He rubbed his forehead. "I just wanted to contribute, you know? Jules — she's got the moves. You've got the brains. Izzy's got the hack. What do I have?"

"You've got the courage," March said.

There was a small silence that March was not tempted to fill. A little space for them to come together without saying a word.

Darius gave a heavy sigh. "We've got to do this, bro."

"What?"

"I stay. You go."

67

ONE SHOT

March's mouth dropped open. "Are you crazy?"

"Listen. It's our only shot. I can't fit through that window, and no way can we get past those guys at the front. Besides, I can't leave, knowing they'll go after Mikki. You and Izzy and Jules, too. We've got to find a way to get them in jail, or deported."

"How? I told you, *I don't know what to do.*" March's voice cracked with exhaustion and despair.

"You do." Darius laid a heavy hand on his shoulder. "What do you always say? 'Break it down.' You got a fractured group, brother against brother. Zef doesn't trust Blue, he's mad at Dmitri for bringing her in. So. You got greed and suspicion. You got a federal agent trying to make his career. You got Blue pretending she's a pop star. You got a greedy billionaire who doesn't care who gets him what he wants, as long as he gets it. And I got this." Darius pointed to a heating vent. "Do you remember that time we were in the kitchen, planning Jules's birthday party? She was in here, heard about the pony, came storming upstairs, and called us idiots."

"Like I could forget."

"I can hear them," Darius said. "The brothers fight like junkyard dogs. Sometimes they speak English, especially if Blue is here. Think about it. Dukey wants to bust them wide open. What if we could give him the key?"

For a long moment, March stared at Darius while options clicked in his head. "We'd have to control the transfer."

"You've got what everyone wants. You set the rules."

"But they can't know it's me. Ransome — we can tell him where the deal needs to go down. He'll listen because he needs the last stone."

"Blue's the contact. She's running the deal. Ransome doesn't even know about the Top Cats."

"Even better. That means they'd have to bring you close to the deal, so Blue can get the last stone from me and get to Ransome in time. If Dukey was in the mix somehow . . ."

Darius nodded. "You got more than you think, is my point. Now give me your phone. They already searched me, they won't do it again. If I'm lucky — and I am Mr. Lucky, Marcello — I'll hear what's going down, and I'll text you."

Slowly March shook his head. "I'm not going to leave you."

Darius ignored him. "If for some reason I can't text you, Izzy can hack in and track where I am. Look, if you have to give up the sapphire, you can still do that. But if you can think of a way to get it all, it's worth the risk."

"You're not getting this! *Nothing* is worth this risk!"

"*We are.* You're the one who really knows it, too. You know without enough money, we're just grifter kids with no hope. You know we need cash to live on the lam. That's why you were so mad at what I did, that's why you're so scared." Darius sat down and took off his shoes. "You *got* to, Marcello. The only way we'll stay together is if the Cats are out of the United States for good."

March swallowed against the fear.

"There is no way I'm leaving you here," he said again.

"We're out of options. And you know I'm right." The worried look left Darius's face as he flashed a grin. "Izzy's gonna punch you."

"Why?"

Darius reached out and snapped his handcuff onto the pipe. He banged it with the metal and yelled, "Hey! I gotta pee!"

"What are you doing?" March whispered furiously.

"You've got about a minute before a goon comes down that hall," Darius said. "Go. But toss me your pick."

March tossed him the pick and the phone.

"I have faith in you, brother," Darius said simply, and March felt his heart seize up as he turned and ran out the door.

68

LOSING IT, FINDING IT

The tears started when he made it out to the street and hit West Broadway. The sobs came so violently they hurt his chest. When had he last cried like this?

When he'd lost Alfie.

How could he have left Darius? How could he have not persuaded him? Should he go back?

His friend, his brother. He'd failed him.

He leaned over, hands on his thighs, trying to stop.

He had to find the courage that Darius had. He had to get control and make this work.

He headed south toward the Brooklyn Bridge. The streets were grayer now. Taxis rumbled by. Sleek dark chauffeured cars slid through the intersections like sharks, maybe carrying finance guys and lawyers heading to work so they could make an extra million on a Sunday. Alfie would say, *It's all the same game. Except we're honest.*

Sometimes needing his father was something so big it blocked out the sky.

Get rid of the fear first. That's the only way you can break it down, bud.

Okay, Pop.

Darius believed in him. And he'd given him something to work with. He had to get the plan straight, or he'd never be able to face Izzy and Jules. He had to do it for Darius.

The sun was rising as March hit the Brooklyn Bridge. He went through it all in his head from the beginning.

If you can't figure the con, think about the players.

Blue, Dmitri, Zef.

Dukey.

Ransome.

Thinking about every word they said. Thinking about what each of them felt. What each of them wanted most. The sun splashed the river with gold. What did Alfie used to say?

Another day to get it right.

He crossed the bridge and kept on walking.

The cobblestones were wet with morning as he pushed open the door to Joey's garage. Izzy and Jules were up, pacing, tense and angry.

"Where were you?"

He dropped, exhausted, on the floor.

"We're going to need a bigger con," he said.

69

WE ARE US

Izzy pounded on him with her fists. "You *left* him there!"

"I had to! He wouldn't come!"

"But you just left him!"

"I had to! There was no way to get him out!"

"I don't care!"

"Ow! Iz, stop punching me! Darius said you'd do this!"

"I'm going to punch him, too! And then I'm going to kill him!"

March caught her wrists gently. "We're going to get him back."

Izzy's adorable face crumpled. "You promise?"

"I promise. I told you the plan. It just has a few holes. If we're lucky, Darius can fill them."

"We can pull this off. I know it," Jules told Izzy.

"Fact: Blue is *scared* of the Top Cats," March said. "I saw her face on that roof. Fact: Zef has been working on Dmitri not to trust her. Fact: Dukey's career would get a huge boost if he kept the Top Cats out of the country. Fact: We've got the sapphire. That gives us power. The Top Cats don't like loose ends? We're going to tie everything up in a nice neat bow for them."

March let out a breath. This was the biggest risk he'd taken since Alfie had died, and that was saying something.

"We only have a little time, and we've got to make it count. We're going to get Darius back, and we're going to get rid of the Top Cats and Blue," March said. "We're going to make it so they leave us alone forever. And we have to go straight. For good this time."

"We do?" Izzy asked. "I don't know if Darius will like it."

"He will. He's not Mikki. He's not his dad. And, Jules, you're not Blue."

Jules's eyes filled with tears. She brushed them away, almost angry.

But not at him.

"I know."

He turned to Izzy. "Your parents aren't coming back."

She bit her lip. "I know."

"And I'm not Alfie," he said. "I can stop."

70

IMAGINE

Shopping List:
Three yellow Mini Coopers

Dukey had agreed to meet them in a place of their choosing, and to come alone. He'd agreed to not wear a wire. He'd agreed to every condition, but how did they know he didn't have a net of agents ready to close around them?

They didn't.

They took the subway to West Eighty-First Street. When they got out, they took a moment to gaze at the grand entrance to the American Museum of Natural History. It had been the first heist that March had planned and executed on his own, and everything had gone wrong, but they'd still made it out with the jewel they'd come for. If his luck would just hold, one more time.

He kept going over the plan in his head. This morning he and Jules had studied maps of Prospect Park, then taken the subway there and walked the route. Discussing every possible thing that could go wrong. Then they were so shaky they had to eat a bag of cookies.

Meanwhile Izzy tracked Darius on GPS. Still at the house. She couldn't text him, but she waited for any texts he might send.

Dukey was the crucial piece. Hamish was waiting, ready to go to Ransome.

"Is it too early for a hot dog?" Izzy asked.

"Yes."

Her phone buzzed. "Darius!"

They all crowded around.

Ask Dukey abt Agent Chernoff. She's on his team. Taking payoffs from TCs.

"Excellent," March said. "That will clinch the deal."

Izzy split off, heading south. She would make slow circles around the area, looking for cops. Only when she gave the all clear would March and Jules move in.

March and Jules sat on the steps of the museum. They waited until the text from Izzy came through. Then they crossed the street and headed south. They crossed into Strawberry Fields and made their way through the tourists snapping photos of the John Lennon memorial. They stood for a moment, pretending to admire IMAGINE spelled out in mosaic.

"He's late," Jules said after a few minutes.

"No. He's here," March said. "He's just checking the area. Like we did."

In another two minutes Dukey ambled into view, wearing khaki pants and a polo shirt under a brown jacket. He carried a takeout cup of coffee. The guy really had to learn how to not telegraph the fact that he was a cop. A skinny guy on the edge of a bench caught sight of Dukey and silently, casually moved off.

Dukey sat down next to Jules. "So. I'm here. I said I was out of favors."

"Yeah, I know," March said. "But I figured you'd make an exception for the chance to bust the Top Cats wide open."

"And how would I do that?" Dukey sipped his coffee, his eyes on the tourists.

"You'd have in custody their top operative in the United States, and I think this person would drop a dime on all of them."

"Who?" Dukey took another sip. "And how?"

"Not so fast," March said. "I have some conditions."

"I don't do conditions. Especially with kids I'm about to bust into juvie."

"Even kids who know which agent of yours is on the take with the Top Cats?"

Only the split second of hesitation told March that Dukey was hooked. "Why should I believe you?"

March said nothing. *If you've baited the hook well enough, there's no need to yank it.*

"Give me a name or there's no deal."

"Chernoff."

Dukey looked at him. He couldn't quite hide his shock. "She's my best agent."

March shrugged. "Go ahead and trust her, then."

"Give me time to check it out."

"We don't have time. It's today or nothing."

"Then nothing."

"Fine." March got up and walked off.

He followed the path a little way and turned back. He could see that Dukey was nettled, and Jules leaned in, talking to him. She was telling him that the American contact was Blue. She spoke, leaning in, then eased back and listened, nodding intently. Finally she smoothed her left eyebrow.

March walked back.

"Let me hear the conditions," Dukey said.

Prospect Park
   3 p.m. today
   Zef will be in front seat, say I'm in the trunk
   I'll be in the car a block ahead w Dmitri & guards
   Blue in Mini nearby waiting for stone
   Blue meeting Ransome alone Rev War monument,
guess you fixed that

Izzy looked up, smiling. "Darius is crushing it."

March nodded. "He always does."

That afternoon they stood in a tight circle, shoulders touching.

"If anything goes wrong —" March started.

"You can't start a pep talk with 'if anything goes wrong,'" Jules interrupted. "You're casting doubt on the whole thing. Making us nervous."

"I'm not casting doubt. I'm just saying, get away if you can," March said. "There's no reason for *all* of us to get caught."

"Yes, there is," Izzy said. "We're in this together. All the way."

Jules nodded. "Now *that's* a pep talk."

"I just want to point out," March said, "that I'm supposed to give the pep talk. That's how we roll."

"Give it up," Jules said. "Izzy's the one who keeps the faith."

"I'll go with that," March said. "Let's go get our life back. Potato chips and ketchup."

"Big Stupid Hollywood Movie Night," Izzy said.

"Meatless Mondays," Jules said. "With pepperoni for Darius."

They all smiled.

"Let's go get our family back," March said.

71

THE DEAL GOES DOWN

It was a beautiful September Sunday, and Prospect Park was crowded with lively energy. Kids, dogs, couples, moms, dads, skateboards, bicycles, soccer balls, and roller skates. A mom and dad swung their toddler between them. A couple shared a frozen lemonade while a wedding party made their way up to the Picnic House, a mariachi band trailing behind. The bright music rose and tangled in the leaves.

It was a perfect day for a double cross.

The players were in place. It was too conspicuous to use earpieces this time, so March had to rely on everyone's split-second timing. He glanced at his new burner phone as they each checked in. Hamish. Mikki. Jocy.

March, Jules, and Izzy walked along the curving drive that led along the lake. It was just as the text from Dmitri had said they'd see: a black SUV sat idling a couple of hundred yards away. They were supposed to walk up to it to make the deal with Zef.

They ignored it and turned left. Down the road another SUV was parked, half-hidden under some trees. Just where Darius said it would be. Beside it was a yellow Mini. They walked up and stood outside the passenger window of the SUV.

A smoked-glass window slid down. The burly driver stared straight ahead. In the passenger seat a familiar-looking man smiled at March.

"You still like breaking rules," Dimmy said.

No, *Dmitri*. The puppy-dog look was gone, the vague happy smile. It was replaced by sharp intelligence and the mild amusement of a man who could flip in one second to titanic rage. The baggy T-shirt and shorts had been replaced by a sharp gray suit and dark tie.

"Hey, Dimmy," March said softly. Pressure was in his head, hot anger racing through his veins, but he had to stay as cool as a floating iceberg. "Thought you loved Florida, like pretty girl's braid, hanging down from A-mer-i-ca."

"Still a funny boy. I prefer Dmitri."

"So, *Dimmy*, why would I go to the other car, when Darius is in this one?"

The door to the Mini opened. Blue stalked over. "I don't have time for games. You've been in my way one too many times. Give me the sapphire."

In the side mirror, March saw the other SUV approaching from behind. Zef must have seen them. Good. He'd expected him to.

"You know there's no cars allowed on this road, right?" March asked.

"Rules are not for me," Dmitri said with a shrug.

"So let's make the deal. First, let me see Darius."

"He's in the trunk. Let me see the stone."

March reached into his pocket. His fist closed around the stone. He withdrew his hand slowly. The black SUV had slid forward and was now pulled up behind Dmitri's car. He could see Zef in the driver's seat.

He opened his palm and held up the stone against the sky, blue against blue.

He snapped his fist closed again.

"I need to examine it," Dmitri said. "Who do you think you're dealing with?"

"Let me see him or no deal," March said.

"You are a very foolish boy," Dmitri said. His gaze was flat. "You want your friend to end up in that lake? You, too, with your pretty girls? Very easy to do."

March swallowed against the dead menace in Dmitri's tone. "Lots of people around."

"You think that matters? My boys are quick."

He put his hand in his pocket. "Darius or no deal."

The rear window slid halfway down. Now March could see Darius in the backseat between two very large men.

"Don't worry, I can take them," Darius said before the window slid up again.

Dmitri tapped his fingers on the car door. "I am surrounded by comedians."

Izzy took a step toward the car. "Don't you hurt him," she said. "Or . . ."

"Or what, little sparrow, you will peck me with your beak?" Dmitri flicked a finger at Izzy, as though she were a fly. "Be quiet."

Izzy threw herself up against the car, inches from Dmitri's face. "I am really tired," she said through her teeth, "of people telling me to be QUIET!"

"Dmitri, ignore them," Blue said. "Just get the stone! I've got an appointment to keep."

"Hand over the sapphire," Dmitri said. "Or we drive away. And I don't think you want that. My men don't like your Darius."

"I want Darius out of the car," March said. "Then you get the stone."

He heard the sound of the lock flipped up. The door opened. Darius got out, his hands handcuffed in back of him. The big guy was there, too, holding him by the upper arms. The door stayed open. It would only take a quick shove to get Darius back in the car again.

"Okay," March said. He dropped the stone into Dmitri's open hand.

"Dmitri?" Blue held out her hand. Dmitri held the stone, examining it.

"They wouldn't dare give us a fake," Blue said.

Dmitri shrugged and dropped the sapphire into Blue's hand. "Go."

Blue took off, rapidly walking to the Mini. She started the car and drove off.

March concentrated on the sounds of the park. A bicycle whizzing by. A child far away shouting in happiness. And the sound of a car accelerating.

"Naturally we will keep your friend until we know the stone is real and the deal goes through," Dmitri said. "Maybe you get him back. Maybe not."

March touched his eyebrow. "Mikki's going to be here at six o'clock."

"What do I care? We'll be gone."

Dmitri made a quick movement with his hand, and the big guy started to muscle Darius into the backseat.

Darius was out of the handcuffs in a second. The guard grabbed for him, surprised, just as a turquoise T-bird screamed down the street, swung in a wide fishtail, and slammed into the back of Zef's car.

"NOBODY MESSES WITH MY BOY!" Mikki screamed.

72

DON'T MESS WITH MIKKI

The impact sent Zef's car crashing into Dmitri's. The air bags inflated. Dmitri ended up with a face full of plastic. White powder clouded the air, released with the deployed air bag. Dmitri howled, unable to move. The driver tried to get out but couldn't open the door.

Meanwhile Darius had been ready. Before the collision he'd already pushed away from the startled bodyguard, who lost his grip when he'd been hit by the open door. Darius had leaped out of the way, rolling on the sidewalk and rising in one fluid move.

Mikki blew a kiss at Darius as she reversed, wheeled the car around, and took off.

"Awesome wheelman move," Jules said.

The air bags were deflating. Pushing it out of the way, Zef was trying to start his engine.

"Time for phase two," March said. "RUN!"

They raced back the way they came, then up the road toward the meeting spot, a Revolutionary War monument. Up ahead, a yellow Mini was pulled over, blocking the jogging trail.

Blue exited the car and walked the short distance to the monument. They stopped at the tree line, waiting.

"They won't chase us?" Darius asked.

"Ransome doesn't know about them. They won't risk the deal," Jules said.

"You'd think Blue would worry about a ticket, parking like that," Izzy said.

"She thinks Chernoff is keeping away the cops," March said. "Actually, it's Dukey. He's on the other side of the hill."

Darius dusted off his pants. "Don't know that I like being this close to the FBI, Marcello. Not a fan of captivity."

"Dukey is waiting for our signal. He wants Blue, and he wants the payoff money. Here's how it will go down. Hamish told Ransome that Blue is going to try to pass off a fake sapphire. Ransome agreed to come in a Mini."

"*The Italian Job*," Darius said.

"Exactly," March said.

The Italian Job was an old British caper movie. One rainy afternoon, March and Darius had watched it three times in a row. In the movie, the crooks steal a bunch of gold and then escape by all driving Mini Coopers through the traffic-clogged streets of Turin.

"The money is in the trunk," March explained. "He and Blue are supposed to exchange cars after he gets the jewels."

"She's going to drive away with our money?"

"She's not going to get the chance. If this works."

"Don't say *if*," Darius said. "I don't like the if."

"When."

"That's the word I like."

Another yellow Mini pulled up. Ransome got out, carrying a brown box. "There's our mark," March said. "He followed instructions. Izzy, send Dmitri our message."

Ransome reached Blue, and the kids walked forward to the monument. When Blue saw them, her face hardened.

"I think you might want to reconsider what's about to go down," March said to Ransome. "She's about to cheat you."

"So I hear," Ransome said.

"Get lost," Blue snapped at March. She reached into her pocket and brought out the jewels. Three sapphires flashed blue fire.

March reached into his own pocket and held up a gem. The gem was bluer than blue, more blue than the sky or the sea. "The Morning Star," he said.

Ransome turned to Blue. "I'm waiting."

Blue turned on March. "You little cheat!"

"It's simple," March said. "Either your stone is real, or mine is." Actually, Blue's stone was real. If something had gone wrong back at the car — if Dmitri had insisted on authenticating it on the spot, for example — it would have to be genuine or they never would have gotten Darius back.

Now it didn't matter which one was real. It only mattered that Ransome didn't know.

"Tell your little friend I need a solution, fast," Ransome said to Blue.

Blue glared at March. "He's no friend of mine."

"If we start looking for friends of yours," Jules said, "we'd have to do a worldwide search, and we'd *still* come up empty."

"Who am I supposed to believe?" Ransome looked from March and Jules to Blue.

"You're the one who came to me," Blue told Ransome, switching to her rich, hypnotic tone. "You know you can trust me."

"I don't trust any of you!" he yelled. "You're thieves!" He shook his head. "Hamish tells me to come in a yellow car, I come in a yellow car. He says there's a fake stone, but the real one will be there, too." He sounded almost petulant. "This was supposed to be easy."

"I have an easy solution," March said. "Take all four."

"Fine. You lot can fight over the money," Ransome said. "Once I get the stones inside my boxes, I'll know if they're real."

Blue smiled. She thought she'd won. She knew that the Top Cats were nearby. March and the gang wouldn't get far if they tried to leave with the money.

But right now March's fingers weren't itching to scoop up the cash. He wasn't thinking every minute about the fortune sitting in a car trunk. He was thinking about the posse around him. He was determined that every step they took would remove the Top Cats and Blue from their lives. Protect Mikki. Protect them all.

Ransome laid out seven boxes on the grass as a white panel truck pulled over in the bicycle lane. A sign on the side read BABYSMART BABYSAFE. The driver began to reverse, then go forward, trying to ease onto the grass. He pulled up and parked, now blocking the Minis from view.

Blue and Ransome didn't notice. Blue watched Ransome intently as he carefully scooped the stones into the smallest box, then placed it inside the next, and the next.

They heard the squeal of a truck door being rolled up. Joey Indiana appeared a minute later, carrying two strollers and dumping them on the grass. Back and forth he went, steering more strollers onto the lawn and lining them up.

Ransome closed the seventh box.

Suddenly the air grew blurry and thick, as though it was full of water. The tree in front of March shimmered and seemed to crackle. Izzy's braid rose straight in the air. March felt someone — some*thing* — brush his shoulder. Static electricity made every hair on his arm rise. A sudden push propelled him forward, and he stumbled. Ransome gripped the box, his knuckles white. His comb-over uncombed, flapping in a sudden breeze.

Then whatever — *whoever* — was gone, rushing into a vacuum that left them stunned and blinking.

Even Blue looked unnerved. She took a shaky step backward.

"Zillah's gone," Izzy said to Ransome. "The stones are reunited."

"Hand over your keys," Blue said to Ransome, sounding rattled. She tossed her keys to him.

"Motor's running," Ransome said. He hugged the boxes to his chest and jerked his head toward the cars, now visible next to the white truck, which had pulled forward a few feet. Joey continued to unload more strollers, and a small crowd had gathered. "I've got my luck back. I don't care who gets the cash."

73

A CHOICE FOR BLUE

Blue dashed toward Ransome's car. She opened the trunk and peered inside.

March and the gang walked leisurely down toward her. She gave a thumbs-up to Dmitri, who was glowering in the SUV across the street. Even from this distance they could see his face was bright pink from the impact of the air bag.

"Free strollers!" Joey shouted. "Get 'em while they're hot! I mean, they're not hot in the stolen sense. Just a free promotion from SafeBabySmartBaby! Or should I say SmartBabySafeBaby!"

Joey had dropped flyers about the free offer in apartment buildings all over Park Slope and Prospect Heights. Brooklyn was full of young parents, expecting parents, and people looking for a deal. More and more of them arrived, some of them hurrying. There was some pushing involved.

The gang reached Blue just as she opened the driver's door. "I can't believe you thought you could beat me," she said. "Give it up, will you? If I were you, I'd take off. You're not very popular with my friends."

"There it is!" A couple holding hands hurried toward the truck. The woman was pregnant. More couples began streaming toward them.

"What is this, a Mommy and Me class?" Blue asked. "Move it!" she yelled at the pregnant women browsing the strollers. They were blocking her car. She leaned inside the car and hit the horn.

"Noise pollution!" a pregnant woman yelled. She patted her belly in a meaningful way.

Blue leaned on the horn again, longer and harder.

"Not so fast, Auntie," Jules said. "We want to show you something first."

"The Top Cats aren't the only ones with an interest in that cash," March said. "The FBI is pretty interested, too."

For the first time, worry creased Blue's face. Her gaze flicked past them.

"Don't worry, they're not here. Yet. They think the deal is going down up over that hill. We still have a little time to chat."

"Before you head back to Dimmy, you might want to check this out." Jules held up her phone. She hit the Play button.

Jules and Dukey sat on a bench in the shot. From that distance, she looked exactly like Blue. She was half-turned, dressed in a frock coat and leggings, her hair streaked with blue dye.

"That's not me," Blue said. "That's you."

"You know that, and I know that . . ." Jules said. She turned up the volume.

"So we have a deal?" Dukey asked. *"You'll hand over the money?"*

"Deal," Jules said. *"As long as you protect me from the Top Cats."*

"Saul Dukey, FBI," March said in answer to the question Blue wasn't asking.

"But it's not me!" Blue said. "He may have thought it was me, but what difference does it make?"

"Oh, Dukey knew it was me," Jules said. "That's not your problem."

"*Dmitri* thinks it's you," March said. "Izzy just sent him the video."

Blue's face became a mask, but he saw the fear behind it.

"He already doesn't trust you," Jules said. "Zef got to him. Imagine how they feel right now."

Darius spoke up. "And Dukey knows that you bribed Chernoff. So you can't skate away from the feds, either. If you deliver that money to the Top Cats, the FBI is going to come charging down that hill."

"You're kinda stuck," Izzy said. "But you deserve it."

Blue swallowed.

"You have a choice," Jules said. "Walk up the hill to the feds, or down the hill to the Top Cats. I'd go with the FBI if I were you. Their methods aren't quite so . . . extreme."

"And let you take off with the cash? You're crazy!"

March shrugged. "'If you don't have a choice, take it.'"

"Look around, Blue," Jules said. "You lost your backup. You always seem to operate with it. But now you're really alone."

Blue pushed Jules aside and got in the car. "Then I'm alone with fifty million dollars."

Agent Dukey appeared through the trees. Several agents stood next to him.

"THIS IS THE FBI!" The voice came through a bullhorn.

"Oops!" Joey called. "Got to be going, folks!"

The people clamoring for strollers began to melt away. One man took off running, leaving his pregnant wife, who screamed "SPIKE!" after him. Some of them grabbed strollers as they ran. Joey dropped the last strollers on the grass and ran back toward the cab of the truck.

Blue gunned the motor. The car accelerated, smashing an empty stroller, then wailed down the road.

"She's taking off with the cash!" Darius yelled.

A dark sedan suddenly tore out of the underbrush and sped after Blue, blocking her escape. FBI agents began running down the hill. A trio of agents split off and headed for March and the gang. Hampered by pregnant women and men pushing strollers, they had to bob and weave their way toward them.

"DON'T MOVE!" Dukey yelled at them.

"Looks like Dukey doesn't trust us after all," March said. "Come on!"

74

FOUR YELLOW MINIS

The Top Cat SUVs took off, rocketing down the park lane. A police car started after them, siren wailing.

In the driver's seat of the truck, Joey hit the gas. The truck pulled out, revealing another yellow Mini, engine running.

"Where did that come from?" Darius asked.

"Joey had a spare Mini in his truck," March said.

"But —"

"Misdirection," March said as they raced toward the car. "The first rule of a con. Blue wanted the money. Ransome wanted the gems. Nobody was looking at Joey. D, you're our wheelman."

Darius slid into the driver's seat, and March, Izzy, and Jules tumbled inside. As they squealed out of the parking lot, two more yellow Mini Coopers jumped forward from behind the trees. All the cars took off in a group, heading for the park exit.

Two dark sedans suddenly made U-turns on the park road and came after them.

"FBI," March said. "Dukey's in the front car."

"Who's in the other Minis?" Darius asked.

"Hamish is driving one, your mom's got the other," March said.

"Oh, man. Hamish is a terrible driver."

"It's okay," March said as another Mini squealed around a corner, practically on two wheels. "We've got Joey's Heather, too. She used to be a NASCAR driver."

Darius blew through a yellow light to exit the park. They plunged into Brooklyn traffic. Behind him the two other yellow cars peeled off. The sedan stayed with them.

"Not good," March said.

"Mama's got it covered," Darius chortled as Mikki returned and cut in back of them.

Izzy studied her phone. She'd gone over and over the route, investigated traffic patterns, planned for obstacles. They'd timed it out early that morning. "Make a right at the light!" she cried, and Darius spun the wheel.

March hung on to the seat as Darius weaved through traffic. He reached across the seat and grabbed Jules's hand. They hung on.

The car careened around corners as the other yellow Minis appeared and disappeared. Now they were in a warehouse district. The other FBI cars had disappeared, but that one black sedan was still one block behind them.

"Dukey," March said. "Such a stubborn guy."

"LEFT!" Izzy shouted.

"Here?" Darius yelled. "It's illegal!"

"Are you serious?" Izzy thumped him hard on the arm. "GO!"

Tires screaming, Darius made a sharp and highly illegal left turn across traffic. He zoomed down a cobblestone street. A white panel truck was parked near the end of the block. The side panel read FAST XPRESS: *YOU DREAM, WE DELIVER.*

The back door rolled open, and two metal planks shimmied down.

"That's Joey's truck. Go!" March shouted.

Darius shifted into second and drove up the planks. He hit the brakes hard, right in front of a magnetic sign reading BABYSMART BABYSAFE.

Joey bounded past them and pulled up the planks. The rear door rang down again. A minute later they heard the sound of a car zooming by, rattling on the uneven cobblestones.

"All clear," Joey said softly.

Darius rested his head against the wheel. He let out a shuddering breath. "I know one thing. I'm not born to be a wheelman."

"Mikki and Heather can handle the rest," March told him. "They're probably in Pennsylvania by now. The feds and the police will follow every yellow Mini they see. They don't want to lose the money."

"And Blue is going to sing all about the Top Cats to Dukey," Jules said. "In handcuffs."

Izzy leaned toward Darius. "You done good, smart baby safe baby," she said.

"We all done good," Jules said.

"Too bad we missed out on the cash," Darius said.

March grinned. "You sure about that?"

EPILOGUE
HOW TO REBOOT

"Just came to say good-bye," Hamish said. "This time, I'm really retired."

March opened the door wider, and he walked in, his arms full of packages. "Bagels, cream cheese, smoked salmon, and a big chocolate babka for you."

"Wow," March said, taking the packages from him. "You shouldn't have done all that shopping."

"I didn't! I cleaned out my refrigerator! My flight leaves at two. I've got a cab waiting downstairs. I can run the meter! I'm a millionaire!" Hamish looked around the place. "I like the new apartment. Not as grand, but nice."

"Thanks." There was no climbing wall, no garden, no yacht, and no pool. The apartment was just big enough for them. Very low profile. They liked it that way.

"Love the decorating scheme," Hamish said.

"Yeah, Joey gave us a deal on beanbag chairs," March said.

"Sorry I ever called that boy an idiot. The way he switched out those Minis so Blue got the fake cash and you got the fortune! Slid that car right out of the truck. Like butter! And Heather missed her calling as a wheelman. Ack. Did I tell you? The two of them used their cut to put Heather through culinary school. They moved upstate," Hamish said. "I always thought Joey would end up upstate, but I thought it would be behind bars. How's Mikki?"

"Still in Florida buying lottery tickets," March said.

"And you've gone straight. Terrible loss of a cunning criminal brain." Hamish sighed. "Best gang I've ever worked with."

"I'm not Alfie," March said.

Hamish put his hand on March's shoulder. "No. You're not. Still, you can't get too comfortable. Dukey could decide to come after you."

"He could. He didn't recover Ransome's money. But he broke the Top Cat case wide open," March said. "Blue is in prison. I think we're square if we stay out of trouble. He didn't look too hard."

"Stealing is such a bad habit. Worse than gluten. But just in case Dukey comes around . . . two exits?"

March nodded. "And it's only fifteen minutes to the George Washington Bridge."

"Excellent. Newark Airport, twenty minutes, you can hop a flight to Mexico and find me."

"So Keiko took you back?" Jules fished around in the bagel bag.

"She is the yin to my yang, the butter to my scotch, the kale to my smoothie," Hamish said. "Yes, she took me back. All I have to do is move to Mazatlán. Why not retire? I cleared my debt with Jimmy the Knife. He gave me his guacamole recipe. For my whole new life!"

"A reboot," Izzy said.

"Exactly! Come visit, young yogis. I'm going to give classes — hatha and restorative. Keiko is perfecting her enchiladas. The beach is lovely, the seafood is fresh, and if you change your mind, there's plenty of rich tourists! Heh. Joke!" Hamish glanced at his watch. "Well, I might be a millionaire, but I don't want to pay a fortune for that cab. Farewell, my magnificent friends."

Hamish hugged March, then Darius, then Jules, then Izzy. "So many adventures. How glad I am they're over." He put his hands together and bowed. "Namaste."

As the door closed behind them, Jules started to slice bagels. Izzy scooped the cream cheese into a bowl.

"Do we have any pepperoni?" Darius asked by the refrigerator.

"With bagels? That's gross," Jules said, and the familiar argument began.

March looked out at the river. Things were different. They had hammered out a plan. They'd invested a chunk of the money — safely, this time — after splitting it with Hamish, Mikki, and Joey and Heather. They'd agreed on some homeschooling, "so we all know who Winston Churchill is," Izzy said. Darius was still interested in investing, and he was studying finance at night. Izzy had befriended a student at Columbia and was learning even more about coding.

They were thinking about getting a dog. Just not a stinky one.

People get broken, FX had said. *Sometimes they take that and make themselves strong.*

They'd make themselves strong. Strong like a family should be.

No more heists. No more lies. They weren't their parents. Blue's monstrous selfishness had taught them everything they needed to know about what not to be.

They could have done it without the fortune. But as Alfie used to say, *Everything goes better with cash.*

Living on twenty million might not be easy. But they were willing to try.

ABOUT THE AUTHOR

Jude Watson is the *New York Times* bestselling author of *Loot: How to Steal a Fortune*, which received starred reviews from *Kirkus Reviews* and *Publishers Weekly*. Rick Riordan called it "the perfect summer read." She has also written five books in The 39 Clues series, including Doublecross Book 1: *Mission Titanic*. Under the alias Judy Blundell, she won the 2008 National Book Award for Young People's Literature for *What I Saw and How I Lied*. The Watson crime family lives on Long Island, in New York.